Schwanengesang

FRANZ SCHUBERT *Schwanengesang*

Facsimiles of the Autograph Score and Sketches, and
Reprint of the First Edition

Edited by Martin Chusid

YALE UNIVERSITY PRESS · NEW HAVEN AND LONDON

Published with assistance from the Mary Cady Tew Memorial Fund.

Copyright © 2000 by Yale University.

All rights reserved.

Designed by Sally Harris / SummerHill Books.

Set in Dante type by The Composing Room of Michigan, Inc.

Printed in the United States of America.

ISBN 0-300-08393-9

Catalogue records for this book are available from the Library of Congress and the British Library.

The paper in this book meets the guidelines for permanence and durability of the Committee on Production Guidelines for Book Longevity of the Council on Library Resources.

10 9 8 7 6 5 4 3 2 1

The publisher wishes to thank the Pierpont Morgan Library for permission to reproduce the autograph score of *Schwanengesang* (Mary Flagler Cary Music Collection, Cary 63) and the first edition (Mary Flagler Cary Music Collection, PMC 110); the Archiv der Gesellschaft der Musikfreunde, Vienna, for permission to reproduce Schubert's sketches for "Liebesbotschaft" and "Frühlingssehnsucht"; and the Stadtbibliothek, Vienna, for permission to reproduce the sketch for "Die Taubenpost."

The reproduction on page xxiii was kindly provided by Mr. James Fuld from his copy of the first edition.

For my son, Jeff—M.C.

Contents

Foreword

Of Schubert's three major song cycles, *Die schöne Müllerin, Winterreise,* and *Schwanengesang,* the one that has received the least critical attention is *Schwanengesang.* I have long felt this to be an undeserved gap in the literature, and shortly after founding The American Schubert Institute (TASI) in 1987, I thought of extending our activities beyond performances and symposia, and filling that gap. I conceived the idea of a publication combining the facsimile of Schubert's autograph of the fourteen songs with a volume of commentary from diverse perspectives: those of the performer, the analyst, and the music historian.

After discussing my ideas with Martin Chusid, I asked if he would take charge of such a project. He responded enthusiastically and suggested adding the three extant sketches as well as the attractive and remarkably accurate first edition by Tobias Haslinger of Vienna. Because the Schubert autograph is held by the Pierpont Morgan Library in New York under the curatorship of J. Rigbie Turner, Martin Chusid and I broached the idea to him. He, too, reacted favorably and promised to contribute to the facsimile volume an essay on the provenance of the autograph. At that point a number of leading writers on Schubert were asked to contribute to the accompanying volume, *A Companion to Schubert's 'Schwanengesang.'*

Once the project was sufficiently advanced, we approached Harry Haskell, Music Editor at Yale University Press. The result, now before you, is the first book initiated and sponsored by TASI. It follows our occasional publication *The TASI Journal,* and we look forward to expanding our scholarly activities to deepen both our understanding and our enjoyment of the works of the incomparable Franz Schubert.

Henny Bordwin, President
The American Schubert Institute

Notes on the Provenance of the Manuscript

J. RIGBIE TURNER

The story of the 140-year journey of the *Schwanengesang* manuscript from Schubert's hand to the Pierpont Morgan Library is briefly told. To Walther Dürr's account of the provenance only a few details are added here.[1]

On 17 December 1828, a month after Schubert's death, his brother Ferdinand delivered to the Viennese publisher Tobias Haslinger the manuscripts of thirteen Schubert songs and the last three piano sonatas. To the songs Haslinger added "Die Taubenpost," and in May 1829 he published the fourteen songs under the title *Schwanengesang*. Tobias Haslinger stands out among Schubert's publishers during his last years. As Dürr writes, Haslinger's editions were scrupulously prepared and are distinguished by the exacting attention paid not only to the music but also to dynamic and articulation signs and even the punctuation of the song texts. The *Wiener Allgemeine Theaterzeitung* described Haslinger's edition of the three songs, Op. 80 (D. 870, 871, and 880), as "clear, correct, and pleasant throughout." The high quality of Haslinger's edition of *Schwanengesang* is evident in the facsimile reproduced here.

The manuscript of *Schwanengesang* was acquired, perhaps from the widow of Tobias Haslinger's son Carl, by Johann Nepomuk Kafka, the Bohemian pianist, composer, and collector who once owned the group of Beethoven sketches—now in the British Library—known as the Kafka Miscellany. The manuscript was next the property of Carl Meinert, the noted collector in Dessau, who is listed as owning it in 1884 and 1897.[2] Near the end of 1897 it was bought by the Musikbibliothek Peters, in Leipzig. The Peters Music Library had opened as a public research library in January 1894 on the ground floor of the firm's building. It was founded by Max Abraham, since 1880 the sole owner of the Peters, who lent to the library his collection of music manuscripts and letters. After Abraham's death, in 1900, Peters was run by his nephew Henri Hinrichsen, who also bought music manuscripts and letters and made them available at the library.

Hinrichsen's second son, Walter, joined the firm in 1931. Walter Hinrichsen left Germany in 1936, and in 1948 founded the C. F. Peters Corporation, in New York. He served in the United States Army, as a master sergeant until 1945, then as Music Officer for the U. S. Zone in Germany. On 21 June 1945, the day the American troops withdrew from Leipzig, Hinrichsen met with Johannes Petschull, managing partner of Peters. About the same time, he took some of the music manuscripts that his father and Max Abraham had lent to the Musikbibliothek Peters; he deemed these family property and reportedly planned to put them at the library's disposal when conditions in Germany once again permitted.[3]

In the event, Hinrichsen brought the manuscripts to the United States, probably in 1946, and over the next several years sold many of them through Walter Schatzki, one of the preeminent antiquarian dealers in New York. In June 1950, Schatzki offered the manuscript of *Schwanengesang* to Mary Flagler Cary, who bought it in October. Mrs. Cary died in 1967, and in 1968 the trustees of her estate gave her collection of music manuscripts and letters to the Morgan Library; the *Schwanengesang* manuscript bears the call number Cary 63.[4]

NOTES

1. Walther Dürr, introduction to *Franz Schubert: 'Schwanengesang:' Dreizehn Lieder nach Gedichten von Rellstab und Heine, Faksimile nach dem Autograph* (Hildesheim, 1978), vii. As the title implies, the facsimile omits "Die Taubenpost."

2. Meinert also owned the manuscript of Schubert's *Winterreise*, which he acquired from Carl Haslinger's widow; today it is in the Morgan Library.

3. Norbert Molkenbur, quoted in "Die grosse Politik und die Verlagspolitik: Quellenkritischer Bericht zu Vorgängen im C. F. Peters in Frankfurt und Leipzig," *Neue Musikzeitung* 39 (1990), 34.

4. The Peters-Hinrichsen-Schatzki-Cary nexus accounts for several prized autographs now in the Morgan Library. In addition to *Schwanengesang*, Mrs. Cary bought the manuscripts of Chopin's Mazurka Op. 59, no. 3, and Polonaises Op. 26; portions of Gluck's *Iphigenie auf Tauris*; and part of Handel's cantata *Qual ti riveggio, oh Dio*, HWV 150. (She declined the Mendelssohn Octet, which went to the Library of Congress.) Since Mrs. Cary's death the Morgan Library itself has bought Mozart's concert aria *Misero! o sogno / Aura, che intorno spiri*, K. 431 / 425b; Weber's *Aufforderung zum Tanze*; and Schubert's Impromptus D. 935.

Introductory Remarks on the Autograph, the Sketches, and the First Edition

MARTIN CHUSID

As far as I can tell, this book is unique. It appears to be the first publication to assemble three different types of primary sources for a major musical work in a single volume. Here, facsimiles of the autograph score and the three extant holograph sketches are presented together with a reprint of the first edition, a visually attractive and accurate publication that appeared less than six months after the composer's death.[1]

It seems fitting that the choice of music should be *Schwanengesang,* a compilation containing the final group of Franz Schubert's songs (seven to poetry by Ludwig Rellstab and six to poems by Heinrich Heine) together with the single Lied "Die Taubenpost" (text by Johann Gabriel Seidl), believed by Schubert's contemporaries to be the last he wrote.[2] The fourteen songs were assembled and given the title *Schwanengesang* at the time the Viennese publisher Tobias Haslinger bought them from Schubert's brother, Ferdinand. (According to Otto Erich Deutsch, Ferdinand participated in the selection of the title.)[3] *Schwanengesang* is generally acknowledged to contain some of the finest music Schubert ever wrote, and it provides a fitting vocal counterpart to the wonderful instrumental works completed during the final months of his life: the last three piano sonatas and the C-major String Quintet.

In this introduction, I shall examine the three types of sources in the order in which they appear in this book: first the autograph, then the sketches, and finally the reprint of the first edition. Because the print is unusually accurate for the time in which it was prepared, its presence in this book allows the reader to compare a good printed edition of *Schwanengesang* with the autograph sources.

The Autograph

The *Schwanengesang* autograph at the Pierpont Morgan Library in New York (Cary 63) is actually a composite of two separate, if unequal, manuscripts. The first contains the seven Rellstab and six Heine songs on thirty-four pages (eight bifolios and a single folio, which was later attached to the second manuscript). The initial song, "Liebesbotschaft," is dated August 1828. This first section, by far the larger, has been combined with "Die Taubenpost," five additional pages of music (one fully used bifolio and a second bifolio containing only the final seven measures of the song on the top brace of the first page). Schubert wrote "Oct. 1828" in the upper right-hand corner of the first page of "Die Taubenpost." The single folio ending the first manuscript was undoubtedly pasted to the second at Haslinger's establishment. Now all the pages, including those containing "Die Taubenpost," are stitched together with string along the center folds of the conjugate leaves. The structure and content of the autograph are shown in the table on page xii.

With the exception of the final bifolio, the paper for the autograph, along with the paper for the sketches, has been identified by Robert Winter as emanating from the Welhartitz paper mills in Bohemia. "Sixteen of the last 18 months of Schubert's life were dominated—in so far as paper was concerned—by a single watermark, one that marked the return of the Welhartitz firm, absent since the end of 1823." He also observes, "The most remarkable feature of this type is the gradual and irreversible fading of the watermark to near-illegibility, a phenomenon associated with wear due to extended life."[4] Whatever Winter saw in the 1970s, when he conducted his research at the Morgan Library, is no longer visible now. Other aspects of the *Schwanengesang* paper are, however, verifiable. The format is consistently oblong, as in almost all of Schubert's song autographs and most of his piano holographs as well. The total span (that is, the distance from the top line of the first stave on the page to the bottom line of the last stave) of all but the final bifolio of paper is 19.3 centimeters. The overall dimensions of the paper range from 30.4 to 31.5 centimeters wide and from 23.2 to 24.7 centimeters tall. The variability results from the manufacturing process. In making paper of the size normally used by Schubert, a single large, rectangular sheet was pressed on a mold, folded twice, and cut along one of the folds. Where the cut was made determined whether the paper would be of oblong or upright format. After the folding and cutting, a pair of nested bifolios (a gathered sheet) resulted. Once these procedures had been completed, only the folded and cut edges were even. The two remaining (rolled, adjacent, and uneven) sides account for the variability.

The final bifolio of the autograph, whose paper is different from the rest, bears the only clearly visible watermark in the manuscript. It indicates that the paper was made by the Kiesling company.[5] This biofolio is somewhat thinner than the Welhartitz paper, and the color is lighter, closer to tan than grey. The paper size is approximately 30.5–30.7 by 24 centimeters, and the total span is 20 centimeters. The lines that make up the music staves are a bit thicker than the lines on the Welhartitz paper.

One final observation can be made about the autograph as a whole. Throughout, penciled numbers appear below the piano part. These numbers were doubtless entered at Haslinger's, indicating that the document served as the *Stichvorlage* (printer's source) for the first edition. As a comparison of the autograph and the first edition demonstrates, except when corrected the numbers penciled into the autograph are the same as those at the ends of the braces of the reprint edition.

Corrections and Alterations in the Autograph

The following remarks concerning corrections and alterations in Schubert's autograph of *Schwanengesang* are not all-inclusive. Many of Schubert's corrections need no discussion. They result from simple lapses of attention as he more or less mechanically copied music from an earlier sketch or draft, or they occurred when the composer repeated a measure, phrase, or section he had just written. These corrections are sometimes referred to as noncompositional. Unless such a lapse reveals an earlier musical conception, as with the keyboard echos in "Liebesbotschaft," it is not mentioned.[6]

A majority of the emendations in the autograph may be found in the keyboard part, perhaps because most of the vocal alterations had already been made during the earlier sketching phase, when Schubert concentrated his attention primarily on the voice part. A good many of the "compositional" changes relate to texture. Although the harmony normally remains the same, in several of the *Schwanengesang* songs Schubert enriches the texture with an added part (for example, in "Liebesbotschaft"), or with doublings of preexisting parts. Less frequently he removes doublings from sonorities, as in the closing measures of "Ihr Bild." At other times he alters an inversion of a chord to good effect, as in the first ending of "Ständchen," or in "Die Taubenpost," where a superior bass line results (m. 81). Sometimes a more interesting harmonization occurs to Schubert, as in m. 32 of "Ständchen." Or he thinks of a superior, perhaps chromatic, secondary part, as in "Ihr Bild." Other significant changes result from measures inserted at the beginning of a new section. Such insertions tend to create a more spacious setting, a sense of greater physical or temporal distance. They are especially effective when separating the (usually more pleasant) past from the (frequently unpleasant) present, as in the approach to the middle section of "Der Atlas."

When Schubert does alter the melodic line at the autograph stage, the result is often striking. The discussion of the beginning figure and its varied repeat in "Der Atlas" is one example. Especially noteworthy are the double set of changes at the musical climax of "Die Stadt" (third section) and the stunning new climax in "Der Doppelgänger" at the moment the protagonist recognizes himself as the phantom double.

"Liebesbotschaft"

A number of the alterations in "Liebesbotschaft" are designed to enrich the texture of the keyboard part. The tenor countermelodies in m. 14 (*c'–b–a–b*) and m. 17 (*c'–d*

Fascicle Structure and Content of the Autograph

Fascicle Structure	Contents
1. A gathered sheet (2 nested bifolios, pp. 1–8)	"Liebesbotschaft" (pp. 1–3) "Kriegers Ahnung" (pp. 4–7) "Frühlingssehnsucht" (begins on p. 8)
2. A second gathered sheet (pp. 9–16)	"Frühlingssehnsucht" (continues on p. 9 and occupies most of p. 10) "Ständchen" (begins at bottom of p. 10 and continues through most of p. 12) "Aufenthalt" (begins at bottom of p. 12 and continues on pp. 13–15) "In der Ferne" (begins on p. 16)
3. Two gathered sheets, nested (pp. 17–32)	"In der Ferne" (continues on p. 17 and most of p. 18) "Abschied" (begins at bottom of p. 18 and occupies pp. 19–24) "Der Atlas" (pp. 25–26) "Ihr Bild" (p. 27) "Das Fischermädchen" (pp. 28–29) "Die Stadt" (p. 30 and most of p. 31) "Am Meer" (begins at bottom of p. 31 and continues on p. 32)
4. A single folio pasted to a bifolio (pp. 33–38)	"Am Meer" (ends at top of p. 33) "Der Doppelgänger" (remainder of p. 33 and p. 34) "Die Taubenpost" (pp. 35–38)
5. A single bifolio (p. 39 and 3 blank pages)[a]	(final 7 mm. of "Die Taubenpost" at top of p. 39)[b]

[a] This bifolio is on a different type of paper from the rest of the autograph.
[b] Page 39 is wrongly paginated as 38. The pagination penciled throughout the autograph is not in Schubert's handwriting.

sharp'–*e'*), for example, were afterthoughts. The facsimile shows the cautious and somewhat clumsy placement of the beams for these figures, a kind of tenor part, by comparison with m. 63 (the return of the music of m. 17), where the beams for the thirty-second notes are reversed (that is, they are over rather than under the treble staff). This allows, for the first time in the song, adequate room for the beam of the tenor line.

"Kriegers Ahnung"

The first potentially significant correction in "Kriegers Ahnung" occurs in the last measure of the opening C-minor section. The voice part originally had two quarter rests corrected to the present whole rest with fermata. Did Schubert originally intend to leave room in that bar for the upbeat eighth note now found in m. 29? If so, the composer may have first conceived of the A-flat-major section as beginning without the introductory bar of an arpeggiated tonic chord in the keyboard part. The additional measure helps considerably in separating the dangerous present from the pleasant memory of the past.

In the vocal line at the beginning of m. 61, where tempo, meter, and key signature change, there is a heavily crossed-through correction. Although the original is difficult to read, Walther Dürr suggests that it was a $\frac{2}{4}$ meter signature.[7] If so, Schubert soon realized that he would have to write too many triplets in the new section and switched to $\frac{6}{8}$ meter.

The most interesting emendations in the song concern the vocal part in mm. 90–96. The original version of the passage is shown in Ex. 1a, the final version in Ex. 1b. Note that the striking leaps in mm. 90 and 92 of the first version correspond, more or less, to the leaps in an earlier passage (mm. 64 and 66). The melody at first rose by step to the cadential pitch *e'* (mm. 95–96). But at some point Schubert decided to save the highest pitch (*f''* in m. 90 of the first version) for m. 95, where it occurs twice in the final version. Why the change? Perhaps because of the text. The new shape of the passage throws more weight on the word "manche" of "manche Schlacht" (many a battle). And it is in one of the many battles that the warrior anticipates his death. To accommodate the new melodic line of mm. 94–96, Schubert also altered the keyboard part.

"Frühlingssehnsucht"

Two changes are worthy of comment in "Frühlingssehnsucht." In m. 39 Schubert corrected the last eighth note in the vocal line. Most editors believe the pitch to have been originally *e flat''*, altered to its upper neighbor, *f''*.[8] If this is true, he added at least a modicum of melodic interest to a passage whose significance is primarily harmonic, the tonicization of the region associated with the distant lowered-seventh degree (A-flat major). Furthermore, the passage would now be linked melodically more closely to the ending of strophes 1–4, with its vocal cadence of *e flat''*–*f flat''*–*e flat''* (mm. 50–

Ex. 1a. "Kriegers Ahnung" (orig.), mm. 90–97

Ex. 1b. "Kriegers Ahnung," mm. 90–97

52 and 95–97) as well as the tonicization of A-flat minor. A similar change occurs in the parallel A-flat-major section of the final strophe (m. 129);[9] only now Schubert alters the *e flat''* to *f flat''*, a pitch that reflects well the darker mood of the final strophe.

The composer also revised the right hand of the piano part in m. 46. Except for the first note, originally it had doubled the left hand at the octave above. Thus the top notes had also doubled the voice part. This also implied that the top note of the first sonority in the next measure was *f''* (Ex. 2). The high *a''* in m. 47, then, was also a later addition, and in fact, the original right-hand part for m. 46 makes sense only if *f''* were the original high note of the initial chord of m. 47. That would be the true doubling of the left hand. In all probability Schubert returned to make these changes, and to introduce the *a″* into m. 47, after he had written the final version of the last strophe of the song. There, in the parallel measure, there is a high *a″* in the voice (m. 136), and the altered version of the right hand is written without any sign of hesitation or correction (mm. 136–137).

Ex. 2. "Frühlingssehnsucht" (orig.), mm. 46–47

"Ständchen"

There are two alterations of interest in "Serenade," both refinements of the harmony. During the first ending, the interlude between the two similar strophes of the song, Schubert initially wrote an octave, *G + G′*, as the bass of the subdominant chords in mm. 29a (minor IV) and 33a (major IV). As a result, there is a progression of primary chords moving from one root position to another. By substituting *D* in place of the octave *G*s for the subdominants, the progression becomes somewhat lighter and promotes movement towards the second strophe better.

The harmony of m. 32b was originally a dominant chord in a context implying D minor more than D major. Although there is no third degree present, the *B-flat* neighboring note in the lowest-sounding chord tone of mm. 29b, 30b, and 31b suggests this. As a result, the newly tonicized area of B minor, the most startling harmonic turn in the song, makes quite an effect in m. 33b. But at some late stage in the compositional process Schubert realized that if he reintroduced *B flat* on the third beat of m. 32b, he could then reinterpret it as *A sharp* (the way it is actually written) as an anticipatory leading tone in the new key. This is a small change, but it helps to effectuate the modulation more smoothly than originally conceived.

"Aufenthalt"

Near the beginning of both the prelude and postlude of "Aufenthalt," Schubert originally wrote a half-note *E* for the bottom pitch (mm. 2 and 135); each was then tied to a note of indeterminate length in the next measure, perhaps a dotted-quarter note (mm. 2–3 and 135–136). The alterations to a quarter note and quarter rest, respectively, were made in a fairly unusual manner for Schubert: scraping with a knife followed by pencil correction. Furthermore, the quarter rests do not resemble the composer's usual manner of notation. They are more angular than the composer's normal quarter rests, resembling a backward and somewhat slanted letter *z*. As a result of these peculiarities, I suspect that the changes were not made by Schubert, but rather were instituted at Haslinger's establishment while work was in progress on the first edition. Particularly on the modern piano, accompanists might well prefer the composer's more sustained bass notes.

Elsewhere in the song there is a keyboard interlude in which the composer modulates by way of an augmented-sixth chord from the key of the dominant, B minor, to the relative major, G, for the central section of the song's palindromic structure. In the original version of m. 53 Schubert delayed by a half measure the movement toward the lowest note of the augmented-sixth chord, *e flat*. With the change, the rhythmic timing of that striking sonority is better.

Another harmonic alteration, somewhat more complex, occurs in the song's final keyboard interlude. Schubert is returning from the dominant (B minor) to the tonic (E minor) for the repetition of the opening section. The crucial harmonic turn occurs in m. 108, where the original sonority consisted in the left hand of sustained half notes, *e + g*, and in the right of repeated triplet eighth notes, *c sharp′ + e′ + a sharp′* (the highest pitch approached from a dissonant *b′* as the first triplet of the initial beat). To approach the outer voices in the next measure, *B + b′*, as if they were dominants rather than tonics, Schubert drops the repeated *c sharps′* of the right hand completely and substitutes *c (natural)* for the *e* in the left hand. The result is another augmented-sixth chord resolving in m. 109 to a tonic chord in second inversion in the key of E minor.[10]

"In der Ferne"

The first correction of "In der Ferne" occurs in mm. 1 and 5 of the prelude, and is repeated in the interludes (mm. 30 and 34, and mm. 59 and 63). The sixteenth notes on the third beat were originally thirty-second notes preceded by an eighth-note *F sharp* to which they were joined by a beam. Schubert converted this somewhat aggressive figure into the quieter but more ominous, brooding final version by scraping, probably with the blade of a knife.

Also in the prelude the right-hand octave in m. 3, tied to the same octave in m. 4, was originally *f sharp + f sharp′*, not *g + g′*. Schubert seems to have introduced the melodic figure 5–flat 6–5 at a late stage in the compositional process.[11]

Another change was made in the left hand of the keyboard at mm. 8–9, where the voice begins to sing. Originally there were no *F sharps;* Schubert appears to have added them at a later stage. A similar change was made at the analogous m. 37.

Parallel or direct octaves and fifths have been much discussed in the literature on "In der Ferne" since it was first printed in 1829. (See the extensive discussion of the subject in chapter 4 of *A Companion to Schubert's 'Schwanengesang.'*) Here it is necessary to indicate only that Schubert avoided parallel octave *F sharps* between the voice and the piano in mm. 16 and 45. He also avoided direct fifths in the keyboard part of mm. 16–17, during the change of position from a tonic chord in second inversion to one in root position. As is indicated in the *Companion,* the composer deliberately wrote far more obvious parallel fifths and octaves because the shocking (to Schubert) text, "Mutterhaus hassenden, Freunde verlassenden" (Hating their family home, forsaking their friends), demanded an equally shocking musical event.

There is one additional significant change in the autograph. The measures of rest in the vocal part of strophe three (mm. 76 and 79) and the measure of rest between strophes 3 and 4 (m. 88) were later additions. While writing out strophe 4, the idea of the rests occurred to him—the rests in mm. 91 and 94 were already present in the original—and he returned to strophe 3 to insert them there as well. The result is more breadth at this point in the song.

"Abschied"

This is the longest of the songs in *Schwanengesang,* with much repetition of similar material in both the voice and the accompaniment. It is no surprise, therefore, that the autograph shows a number of lapses of attention. Schubert canceled repeat signs unnecessarily (for example, in m. 38, keyboard left hand) only to write the same notes over the cancellation. At other times he continued a dactylic pattern in the voice important throughout the song, only to discover that he had too few syllables of text for the rhythm. His correction was to cancel the second eighth note and change the first to a quarter note (see m. 68, second beat, and m. 75, fourth beat).

More important were some melodic changes. In m. 24 of the voice part Schubert altered a *g'*, originally written as his last pitch, to *c''* in order to improve the melody. Similarly, in m. 95 he lowered the tessitura of the vocal part; he converted a repeated *e flat''* on the second beat to *b flat'*; and he lowered by an octave the *e flat''* on the final beat. As a result, the arpeggiated ascent to *e flat''* in the next measure now illustrates the text "weit und breit" (far and wide) wonderfully.

"Der Atlas"

Corrections in mm. 4–7 of "Der Atlas" indicate that Schubert had originally conceived the upbeat sixteenth note to the opening motive as *g'* instead of the stronger *d'*

(mm. 4 and 6) and first wrote a literal repeat of that motive for mm. 7–8 (Ex. 3).[12] The varied repeat of the final version is far more interesting.

Ex. 3. "Der Atlas" (orig.), mm. 5–8

Later in the song Schubert inserted a bar of rest for the voice (m. 22) and repeated the piano part for m. 21 to provide more space between the close in B minor, with its text "und brechen will mir das Herz im Leibe" (and in my body, my heart wants to break), and the new section in B major beginning "Du stolzes Herz" (You arrogant heart). Similarly, he added another bar of rest in the voice (m. 27) between the lines of text "du hast es ja gewollt!" (this is what you wanted!) and "Du wolltest glücklich sein, unendlich glücklich" (You wanted to be happy, immensely happy). Again Schubert had to insert repeat signs, this time for the accompaniment of m. 27. Both insertions allow an additional statement in major of the opening figure in the keyboard left hand. The result is more spaciousness, as well as a greater sense of temporal distance between the agony of the present (in G minor and B minor), and the past, when Atlas "wanted to be . . . immensely happy" (in B major).[13]

"Ihr Bild"

In m. 11 of the vocal line in "Ihr Bild" the second note shows a flat sign altered to a natural. Because the B-flat-minor key signature obviates the need for a flat sign, it may be that Schubert began with the natural sign, changed his mind—and the modal orientation of that portion of the phrase—and then returned to his original thought. In the next measure (m. 12) and the return of that bar in part III of the song (m. 34), the left hand of the keyboard began with a dotted half chord, as in the right hand. This was followed by a quarter-note dyad (*B flat* + *A flat*) to complete the measure. At a late stage of composition Schubert added the more interesting chromatic motion of the third quarter (*B flat* + *A natural*) preceded by the *B flat* eighth note to provide emphasis to the new progression.

In m. 34 the composer forgot to enter the natural sign in front of the *A* on the third quarter, but he did enter the flat in front of that note on the last quarter. He may have assumed that he had a key signature of B-flat major at the time. Finally, two sonorities in the keyboard part were reduced. In m. 23 the right-hand chord originally included a *g flat*, and in m. 35 the final chord initially included a *c'* in the right hand and an *e flat* in the left. In both cases the reduced sonority of the final version would seem to be more in keeping with the predominantly thin texture elsewhere in the Lied, a texture that contributes to the dream-like quality of the song.

"Das Fischermädchen"

As with other songs in *Schwanengesang,* Schubert added pitches to the keyboard part of "Das Fischermädchen" for added resonance at a late compositional stage. These pitches usually double another voice at the octave. See, for example, the *e flats* in the right hand at mm. 7–8, as well as the repeated *f* in the left hand at m. 14. In the second case the canceled eighth-note flag on the second *f* makes the addition quite clear. In mm. 7–8 Schubert also deleted a *b flat* in the left hand (m. 7), perhaps to compensate for the added *e flats*. See also m. 70, at which point Schubert appears to have decided on the final version.

Of considerable interest are a number of alterations in the melodic line. In m. 15 the *e flat* on the sixth eighth note of the right hand was initially *f flat*. At mm. 22 and 64 the first three notes of the melodic line were originally *g flat″–f″–e flat″* instead of *f″–e flat″–d flat″*. In mm. 27–28 there were a number of related changes. In the left hand of m. 27, there was originally a repeat sign indicating a continuation of the D-flat-major harmony for the second half of the bar; in m. 28 the first pitches were initially *a double flat′ + d flat′* twice. Schubert then cancelled the repeat sign in m. 27, removed the twofold *a double flat′* in the second half of the measure, and substituted *g flats′* instead. Meanwhile, the melodic line in the right hand at the beginning of m. 28 was altered from *f flat′–g flat′–e flat′* to *g flat′–f flat′–e flat′*. The changes provide a smoother transition to the new key of C-flat major for the second strophe of the song.

"Die Stadt"

The most important corrections in "Die Stadt" are intended to differentiate the voice part of the returning section, section III of the three-part form, from the musically similar but poetically quite dissimilar text of section I. In the process Schubert strengthened considerably the climax of the song. The triplets on the third beat of m. 29 underwent two successive revisions: first there were three *a flats′* altered to *g′–f′–a flat′*; then Schubert wrote his final version: *f′–e natural′–f′*. The larger leap, now a fifth upward in place of a third, emphasizes more strongly the *c″* of m. 30, the high point of the phrase. With a similar purpose in mind, he altered the next phrase as well. This is the climactic moment of the Lied. Schubert raised what had been an *e flat″* in m. 34 (compare the repeated *e flats″* in m. 13) to *g″*, the highest pitch in the vocal part (Ex. 4a shows the original version and Ex. 4b the revision). In the process he emphasized the crucial text "Wo ich das Liebste verlor" (Where I lost my beloved).

Ex. 4a. "Die Stadt" (orig.), mm. 34–35

Ex. 4b. "Die Stadt," mm. 32–35

"Am Meer"

Initially the augmented-sixth chord in m. 1 of "Am Meer" was written with an *e flat* rather than a *d sharp*. The original spelling suggests more strongly a relationship with the diminished-seventh chord so important for the preceding song, "Die Stadt."[14] Why did Schubert change the spelling? Two thoughts occur. The single accidental (*d sharp*) may have seemed preferable to the two successive accidentals required by *e flat* followed by *e natural*. Furthermore, whereas the *e flat* was a diatonic scale degree in the key of "Die Stadt" (C minor), the voice leading of *d sharp* to *e* is preferable in C major, the key of "Am Meer."

In m. 2 of the same prelude originally there seems to have been a fermata above the augmented-sixth chord. Did Schubert intend fermatas over both chords in the measure? Or did he plan just one fermata over the first chord, as in the final bar of the song? Apropos m. 2, initially the composer again seems to have written a whole-note octave (*c + C*), as in m. 1, before he realized that he needed rhythmic space for an upbeat chord to the next measure.

As in the preceding measure, Schubert began to write the keyboard of m. 16 as a tremolo half-note chord. Before completing the sonority, however, he realized that he wanted instead four quarter-note harmonies. He therefore filled in several half-note heads and canceled others so that he could write the exciting and dissonant minor-ninth chord on the second beat. On repetition in m. 37 Schubert wrote the final version cleanly. Finally, the whole-note *g* in the keyboard part of m. 22 was at first a half note, as in the freely imitative next measure.

"Der Doppelgänger"

The first notable correction in "Der Doppelgänger" occurs in mm. 13–15. The upper stave of the keyboard part was originally written in bass clef and began, but never completed, a four-bar ostinato statement rather than echoing the vocal cadence of mm. 11–12. Because there is no change in the voice part of mm. 13ff. and the keyboard echo is written properly (that is, without correction) in mm. 23–24, I suspect a lapse on Schubert's part as he recalled or mechanically copied from an earlier draft of the song. In contrast, there are other songs in *Schwanengesang* where the keyboard echos appear to have been later compositional decisions. See, for example, the corrections in both the continuity draft and the autograph of "Liebesbotschaft."

An even more exciting change may be discerned at the song's climax, the protagonist's recognition of "meine eigne Gestalt" (my own countenance). Originally the vocal part in mm. 40–42 had the same pitches as mm. 31–33 (that is, there was a drop from high *f sharps"* to middle-register *f sharps'*). The earlier version (Ex. 5a), then, essentially duplicated in verses 7–8 Schubert's setting of verses 5–6 of stanza 2. In the final version (Ex. 5b), rising to *g"* — now the highest pitch in the song — provides a far stronger climax than previously. The lack of keyboard music in the cancelled measures indicates that, despite the structural importance of the ostinato-like piano part, in "Der Doppelgänger" Schubert followed his usual practice of writing out the voice part first. Presumably, if he had remained with the earlier vocal line, the augmented-sixth chord would have resembled that of mm. 32–33, that is, it would have been of the French rather than the German variety. Finally, in the voice part of m. 48 the final pitch, the upbeat to the next bar, was originally *c sharp'* rather than *c double sharp'*.

Ex. 5a. "Der Doppelgänger" (orig.), mm. 40–42

Ex. 5b. "Der Doppelgänger," mm. 40–42

"Die Taubenpost"

The first important correction in the autograph manuscript of "Die Taubenpost" is to be found in the left hand of the keyboard at m. 22. Originally the second half of the measure read as in Ex. 6a, recalling the texture of the left hand from the beginning of the song to this point. Examining the final version of this bar (Ex. 6b), we note for the first time triads played by the left hand on the fifth and seventh eighth notes. To enrich the texture at the double cadence (first deceptive, then authentic),

Schubert added a dyad, *g + a*, on the fifth eighth note and also added *d* to the existing dyad of *f sharp + a* on the seventh eighth note. There are similar additions in the repetition of the bar (m. 24). Parallel measures throughout the song (mm. 44 and 46, 68 and 70, 83 and 85, and 98 and 100) show exactly the same kind of (later) enrichment. In almost every case the placement of the beam for the original version just barely allowed Schubert to fit in the *d* (or the *f* in mm. 44 and 46). Several of the dyads added to the fifth eighth note lack stems to the original pitch (mm. 22, 84, and 86), and when the stems are added, they are usually slightly misaligned to the right. The fact that the additions are made to the very end of the song indicates that Schubert opted for the change at a late stage in the compositional process, perhaps when he was adding the dynamic and articulation marks. These are missing from the "Die Taubenpost" sketch and are normally provided by composers during the final phases of composition.

Ex. 6a: "Die Taubenpost" (orig.), m. 22; Ex. 6b: "Die Taubenpost," m. 22

Measure 45 has an interesting correction, again in the left hand of the piano and the second half of the measure. Visible on the facsimile is a natural sign, partially scraped away, on the seventh eighth note. The original harmony, a tonic B-flat triad in first inversion (Ex. 7a), precisely parallels m. 23, where the same music is heard in the key of G major. The facsimile at m. 45 also reveals that all the pitches, as well as the leger lines on which the *e flats* are located, were exaggerated in size by Schubert during the rewriting (Ex. 7b shows the final version). This is a common feature of his corrections made on top of earlier notation. Elsewhere in the manuscript Schubert tends to reduce the length of the leger lines as they ascend above the staff; but the reverse is true here. Whereas the original harmony sounds satisfactory, the new version, a subdominant chord, is fresher.

Ex. 7a: "Die Taubenpost (orig.), m. 45; Ex. 7b: "Die Taubenpost," m. 45

In the right hand of m. 47 Schubert originally wrote once more the descending scale figure in sixteenth notes, perhaps meant to symbolize the pigeon in flight. This musical image appeared in mm. 23 and 45 and reappears later in the song (mm. 69 and 84). The cancelled statement in m. 47, however, would have been the single instance where the idea was immediately repeated, and Schubert decided against it. Because a bar of syncopated chords always follows the scale, the composer wrote one here as well (the original version of m. 48), and it, too, had to be altered.

Of the minor corrections, one may be mentioned, again in the keyboard. Initially Schubert wrote a *G sharp* in the bass on the first beat of m. 81. He then scraped away the note and its accidental and substituted *B*. The new pitch results in a stronger bass line, one that ascends by step from *G sharp* to *e* (mm. 79–84).

The Sketches

The three extant sketches, those for "Liebesbotschaft," "Frühlingssehnsucht," and "Die Taubenpost," represent three different stages in Schubert's creative process and they will be discussed in the order of that process: "Frühlingssehnsucht," the sketch fragment, first; "Die Taubenpost," the continuity draft, next; and "Liebesbotschaft," the skeleton score, last. The briefest of the three sketches, eleven measures of an un-texted vocal line, was identified as belonging to "Frühlingssehnsucht" by Eusebius Mandyczewski, chief editor of the old Complete Edition (completed in 1897), who was also responsible for all the song volumes in that edition.[15] The relatively short, incomplete passage might well be called a sketch fragment, and it represents an early stage of writing not often seen in the manuscripts of Schubert's mature music. The fragment is to be found on the final page of an autograph consisting of a single bifolio and following the more extensive sketch (two pages) for "Liebesbotschaft," first of the Rellstab songs.

The initial page of that bifolio consists of an all-but-completed setting of the first stanza of Rellstab's poem "Lebensmuth" (D. 937).[16] Because all three songs in the manuscript are based on poetry by the author from Berlin, it is generally assumed that at one time Schubert intended "Lebensmuth" as the opening Lied of the Rellstab songs. Although this sketch is consistently called a fragment, there are actually no missing notes in "Lebensmuth." A perfectly satisfactory performance is achieved by adding a set of repeat signs at the beginning of the first complete measure of the prelude, another set at the point where Schubert stopped, and a *fine* at the tonic chord in measure four of the prelude. The musical repeats are then sung with the two stanzas of Rellstab's poem not entered into the manuscript by the young composer. As is often the case with Schubert's strophic settings, the prelude also functions as interlude (here twice) and postlude.[17]

In order to understand the "Frühlingssehnsucht" sketch, it is important to recognize the complex structure of Rellstab's poetry. The first stanza may suffice to make the point.

Säuselnde Lüfte,	[Rustling breezes
Wehend so mild,	Blowing so mild,
Blumiger Düfte	My breathing filled
Athmend erfüllt!	With flowery fragrance!
Wie haucht ihr mich wonnig	How blissfully you breathe
begrüssend an!	greetings upon me!
Wie habt ihr dem pochenden	What have you done to my
Herzen gethan?	throbbing heart?
Es möchte Euch folgen auf	It yearns to follow you
luftiger Bahn!	on airy paths!
Wohin?	Where to?][18]

With the poetry in mind, the fragmentary sketch begins to make sense, if not particularly good music. Schubert set the initial group of four short lines in $\frac{9}{8}$ meter (mm. 1–5). The three longer lines that follow were composed in common time, and the sketch ends before the final, short verse, "Wohin?" The key at the beginning and end of the fragment is D major, and there is a turn to its relative, B minor, at the beginning of the passage in common time. As the fragment develops, particularly in the second part, a vague resemblance to the final version begins to emerge. Notice the dactylic rhythm and arpeggiation toward the end of the sketch (Ex. 8a), which foreshadow mm. 42–45 of the actual song (Ex. 8b).

Ex. 8a. "Frühlingssehnsucht" (sketch), mm. 6–11

Ex. 8b. "Frühlingssehnsucht," mm. 42–49

It seems reasonable to assume that Schubert decided not to proceed further because he found two insurmountable problems at the point he abandoned the fragment.

First, how was he to handle the very short but crucial final line, "Wohin?" Second, what was he to do with the four successive stanzas if he retained the sketch as the basis for the song? The most logical setting for the relatively long poem, and the one Schubert ultimately selected, was strophic. But this would have resulted in a constant shifting back and forth between two quite different musical meters, causing problems for the pacing of the song.

Because the music of the final version is so different from that of the sketch, it is tempting to hypothesize a lost intermediate stage, perhaps a continuity draft in the fashion of "Die Taubenpost" (discussed below). In any case, because none of the Rellstab songs in *Schwanengesang* are in the same key, it may well be that Schubert dropped "Lebensmuth," a song in B-flat major, from the Rellstab group about the same time he decided to change the key of "Frühlingssehnsucht" from D to B flat. Although the fragmentary sketch of "Frühlingssehnsucht" has relatively little to do with its final version, a number of the ideas in that sketch may have reverberated in Schubert's mind during the composition of the next song in the group, "Ständchen."

It is unfortunate that a sketch for "Ständchen," known to have been in private hands in Budapest in 1865, has disappeared.[19] It would have been interesting to know if it had anything in common with mm. 1–5, the $\frac{9}{8}$ section, of the "Frühlingssehnsucht" sketch. Certainly the final version of "Serenade" (Ex. 9b) shares several of the sketch's musical features (Ex. 9a). Both "Ständchen" and the sketch for the previous song begin with a downbeat and share a similar rhythmic configuration for two measures. To its detriment, the melody of the sketch continues with the triplet subdivision on the first beats of mm. 3 and 4, no doubt in response to the repetition of the dactylic metric patterns of the poetry. In m. 3 of the infinitely more beautiful melody of "Ständchen," in contrast, Schubert moves the triplet to the third beat, and there is none at all in m. 4. The underlying rhythmic similarity of the two openings is all the more startling when we realize that the meter of the serenade's poem is primarily trochaic. To obtain the triplets—and they are a consistent feature of the song—Schubert has to introduce a more melismatic setting of the text. The resultant emphasis on melody is quite clearly a function of the poem's meaning. "Serenade" is a song; in opera it would qualify as stage music, that is, the characters in the opera would hear it as music. Whereas syllabic settings tend to favor the verbal aspects and comprehension, melismas favor the musical element. In this case, it is a doubly musical element. Not only is the poem a song, but an important component of the serenader's text is the reference to nightingales singing.[20] In passing it may be observed that musical subjects, or poetic references to music, inspired Schubert to write some of his finest songs. Splendid examples are the final songs of *Die schöne Müllerin* ("Des Baches Wiegenlied") and *Winterreise* ("Der Leiermann"), and "Ständchen" is certainly no exception.

Ex. 9a. "Frühlingssehnsucht" (sketch), mm. 1–5

Ex. 9b. "Ständchen," mm. 5–8

Another feature of the "Frühlingssehnsucht" sketch that may have influenced "Ständchen" is the tonal center D, with its modulation to B minor. To be sure, in the serenade there is a constant and incredibly poignant oscillation between the major and minor modes present neither in the sketch nor in the final version of "Frühlingssehnsucht." Perhaps Schubert wanted the key of D in relation to the previous songs of the Rellstab group. Notice that both early and final groups include the keys of B flat, G, and D (although not in the same order:

Sketch Manuscript	Key	Final Version	Key
"Lebensmuth"	B-flat major	"Liebesbotschaft"	G major
"Liebesbotschaft"	G major	"Kriegers Ahnung"	C minor
"Frühlingssehnsucht"	D major	"Frühlingssehnsucht"	B-flat major
		"Ständchen"	D minor / major

Relatively few sketch fragments for Schubert songs survive. Either he did not put many on paper, or those written down were discarded. We'll probably never know which, unless new pages of fragments come to light. We can, however, ask why he kept the unpromising eleven measures of "Frühlingssehnsucht." Perhaps he did so for the same reason that he kept the abandoned skeleton score of "Liebesbotschaft." Both were on the same bifolio of music paper containing the only manuscript of the all-but-completed song "Lebensmut." In its present form—that is, without a note missing—the holograph of "Lebensmut" could have been handed to a publisher who would have put on the final touches discussed earlier. As a result of the presence of "Lebensmut," then, the bifolio had value for Schubert, and he retained it.

A later stage in the compositional process is represented by the single folio sketch for "Die Taubenpost," corresponding to what has sometimes been called a continuity draft.[21] This type of sketch presents a version of the complete, or virtually complete, music for the vocal part, usually with instrumental interludes to maintain the melodic continuity. Often, as here, the continuity draft lacks the prelude, postlude, and some of the text, and, again as here, more often than not the composer uses fewer staves than are required for the final Lied. In the draft of "Die Taubenpost" there are two staves. On the upper one is a complete version of the voice part, together with the upper part of four keyboard interludes (one hundred measures of music); on the lower stave is a bass part for mm. 1–22 of the vocal part. The last of the four interludes in the draft was omitted from the final version of the song.

Unlike the exceptionally clean sketch for "Liebesbotschaft" (discussed below), the draft of "Die Taubenpost" offers an exciting opportunity to glimpse Schubert in his workshop. There are significant changes in the opening measures of the voice part, and this is the melody returning most frequently in the song. There are also substantial alterations in the interludes and an important change in the harmonic plan of the final section, the climax of the song.

Schubert begins the first phrase of the vocal line with a repetition of the tonic, g', leaping to the dominant, d''. Later he substituted motion from the mediant to the dominant (b' to d''). In the final version this melody is heard four times (mm. 6, 10, 52, and 56).[22] The effect of the tonic beginning (Ex. 10a) is decidedly heavy by comparison with the light, buoyant tone of the mediant, poised, as it were, between the tonic and dominant scale degrees (Ex. 10b).

Ex. 10a. "Die Taubenpost" (draft), mm. 1–8

Ex. 10b. "Die Taubenpost," mm. 6–13

In a correction of the draft corresponding to m. 22 of the final version, Schubert altered three a's on beats 1 and 2, once more to the lighter mediant b's, and changed two quarter-note c''s to d''s on beats 3 and 4. In m. 24 of the draft (m. 23 of the final version) there is a high g'' set to the clumsy interpolated exclamation "Ja" on the fourth beat. For the final version the g'' is deleted, postponed till later in the song (m. 69), where there is a syllable for the note at the beginning of the line of text "Die Taub' ist so mir treu"

(The dove is so faithful to me). The syllable "Die" is underlined by Schubert in the autograph, both here and in the previous measure. The phrases in question are verbally similar, and musically they repeat the setting of the final lines of stanzas 2 and 6.

At the beginning of the second section (the setting of stanzas 3 and 4 of the poem), Schubert improved considerably the melody of the draft corresponding to mm. 30–34 of the completed composition. Again the first note was the tonic, altered once more to the mediant. Furthermore, the melodic line of m. 26 in the draft (Ex. 11a) proves to be considerably less interesting than the final version (Ex. 11b).

Ex. 11a. "Die Taubenpost" (draft), mm. 25–26

Ex. 11b. "Die Taubenpost," mm. 30–31

Schubert made a particularly significant change in the final section. While setting the pivotal line of text "Sie heisst—die Sehnsucht! Kennt ihr sie?" (She's called—longing! Do you know her?) for the second time, he introduced the most distant harmonic area of the song, a tonicized lowered sixth degree (E-flat major). As a result, the tension created by the earlier appearance of the supertonic (A, both major and minor) was further heightened. (Exx. 12a and 12b provide a comparison of the first and second versions of this line.)

Ex. 12a. "Die Taubenpost" (draft), mm. 86–94

Ex. 12b. "Die Taubenpost," mm. 87–95

Notice the lower tessitura of the voice part in the final version. This allows a gradual rise through *f natural″* (m. 96) to *g″* (mm. 99–100), where Schubert made his final melodic improvement. He simplified the rhythm and introduced a new pitch, *e″*, in the second part of the measure (Ex. 13a shows the first version and Ex. 13b the second).

Ex. 13a. *"Die Taubenpost" (draft), 99–100*

Ex. 13b. *"Die Taubenpost," mm. 100–101*

The absence of the wonderfully syncopated accompaniment is, perhaps, the most striking feature of the draft. Together with the dotted pattern on the second part of the measure, and the greatly improved (lightened) melodic line, the accompaniment produces an "airborne" effect that seems to be remarkably appropriate for the image of the pigeon in flight. Also absent from the draft is the descending sixteenth-note figure in the right hand of the accompaniment, the musical counterpart of the pigeon's descent "Bis zu der Liebsten Haus" (Right to my dearest's house). The figure occurs in m. 23 and again in mm. 45 and 99. Walther Dürr has suggested that the keyboard parts in Schubert's songs often provide a kind of musical counterpart for the verbal cues of the scenario, for the stage set and stage directions in an opera.[23] The keyboard part certainly performs this function in "Die Taubenpost."

The changes made to the piano interludes of the draft are particularly striking. As originally conceived, the effect tends to be overly heavy: mainly blocks of chords in a middle register set to dactylic rhythms. In the final version Schubert completely rewrites two of the interludes (mm. 13–14 and 59–60), substituting a combination of syncopations and dotted rhythms. At the same time he simplifies the harmony and eliminates the overly affective augmented-sixth chord in m. 14 (suggested as well in m. 60, although the bass is not written out). Furthermore, in the interlude between stanzas 4 and 5 (mm. 48–51), the weightier dactyls are eliminated in favor of the lighter dotted patterns, and Schubert removes completely the final interlude, which would have appeared after m. 71. In the process he accelerates the motion toward the climactic section of the song. The single interlude still resembling the original (mm. 26–29) loses one dactyl (m. 26), and the two dactyls remaining are single notes rather than chords (mm. 28–29).

The sketch for "Liebesbotschaft," though resembling a continuity draft, represents still another compositional stage, one closer to the final version of the song. Here the layout on the score page (with three staves and a blank space left for the prelude) suggests that originally Schubert intended the continuity draft to serve as a skeleton score. That is, he intended to fill in the missing text (present only for mm. 6–12 in the sketch) and the absent keyboard portions, thereby converting the draft into his autograph. Differences in the colors of the ink on the holograph suggest that Schubert had once also written a skeleton score for "Lebensmut," immediately preceding the "Liebesbotschaft" sketch in the same manuscript. Although there is relatively little notated on the keyboard staves of "Liebesbotschaft," it seems clear that Schubert had his ideas for the piano portion of the song well in mind. This is apparent from the first pair of measures of the draft, where he notates the arpeggiated thirty-second notes in the right hand. To be sure, the precise configuration, and the crucial first notes of each arpeggio—with their implied countermelody—were later altered. In the version we know, there is a more interesting rising chromatic line, *g′–g sharp′–a′*, in contrary motion to the melody, rather than the descending *c″–b′–a′* of the sketch, which parallels the melody. Nevertheless, and this is the crucial aspect, he had already conceived the prevailing flow of thirty-second-notes for the piano, the rushing brook, as it were. The melodies of both interludes are also present, although the first (mm. 30–31) is written an octave higher than in the final version. By shifting the register, Schubert allows the continuous thirty-second notes to remain in the accompanist's right hand throughout the song.

The major difference between the sketch and the final version is the absence of the prelude and the closely related postlude. Some minor differences are also noteworthy. The most common are alterations to the cadential pitches of a number of vocal phrases. In almost every instance Schubert abbreviates the note and inserts a rest. This provides breathing points, which are taken by the singer in any case. For example, the last vocal pitches in mm. 19, 25, and 43 of the final version, eighth notes followed by eighth rests, are written in the sketch simply as quarter notes. There are a number of other similar changes. In one instance, however, Schubert reverses the process. In m. 32 he substitutes a dotted eighth note for an eighth note and a sixteenth rest. The more sustained pitch suits well the text of stanza 3, where the maiden is dreaming.

In m. 42 the voice part was altered to save the *f sharp′*, the high point of that line, for m. 45. And, finally, in m. 59 the composer changed an ornament; he substituted a less fussy grace note *c″* for a short trill on *b′*. In these minor changes, three goals seem to have guided Schubert: to correlate the music better with the meaning of the text (the more sustained pitch in m. 32); to improve some aspect of the musical design (the saving of the *f sharp′* of m. 42 for its repetition); and to ease the performer's task (the provision for breathing spaces at the ends of phrases).

One correction in the sketch is especially intriguing. Originally Schubert omitted m. 8 and its rest. This is the first point at which the piano echos the voice part. Was there ever an early version of the song, perhaps only in the composer's head as he studied the poetry, in which there were no echos? Certainly singing the voice part without the echos makes perfectly good musical sense. At least a partial confirmation of this theory is provided by the autograph. As Schubert was writing the voice part into that document, he again omitted a bar of rest for the keyboard echo. This time it was m. 11, the second piano echo, that was missing, and it had to be inserted later.

Some conclusions about the sketches are in order. It seems clear, if hardly surprising, that when he composed a song Schubert first concentrated on the poetry, probably memorizing the text before putting pen to paper.[24] In the process, he no doubt began thinking of possible melodic ideas for that text. The paucity of such extant fragments as the sketch of "Frühlingssehnsucht" suggests that most of the preliminary casting about for suitable melodies was not recorded on paper. It may have been the complexity of the poetry for "Frühlingssehnsucht" that led the composer to write down his musical thoughts. Ideas for the keyboard accompaniment may also have occurred to Schubert as he reflected on the words, but there is no sign of it in the single line fragment, and little more in the two-stave continuity draft for "Die Taubenpost." In this draft there is only a bass line for the first twenty-two vocal measures, a memorandum for harmonies largely implicit in the voice part itself. Only in the late stage of the skeleton score for "Liebesbotschaft" do we find any accompanimental figuration, and there it is only two measures. Notice how different these measures are from the interludes in "Die Taubenpost" and "Liebesbotschaft," which provide melodic continuity between the vocal phrases rather than accompaniment or counterpoint to the voice. It confirms the primacy of the voice part in Schubert's approach to song composition that not one of the three sketches contains a prelude or postlude.

Finally, some physical characteristics of the sketches are worth noting.[25] The originals of the sketches for "Liebesbotschaft" and "Frühlingssehnsucht" are at the Gesesellschaft der Musikfreunde in Vienna (call number A 236). Both are on a single bifolio in oblong format, which also includes as its first page "Lebensmuth" (D. 937). As noted earlier, "Liebesbotschaft" was probably intended as a skeleton score, and occupies folios 1 verso and 2 recto of the manuscript; the sketch fragment for "Frühlingssehnsucht" is on folio 2 verso.

The paper, without a visible watermark, has been identified by Robert Winter as originating in the Bohemian paper mill of Welhartitz.[26] It measures 31.5 by 24 centimeters with sixteen staves per page and has a total span of 19.4 centimeters. The paper is relatively thin with a tannish tint and has been cut at the top. The ink is brown.

The sketch for "Die Taubenpost," located at the Viennese Stadtbibliothek (call number MH 4100 / c) is a continuity draft on both sides of a single oblong leaf. Again there is no watermark, but Winter claims that the paper is also from the Welhartitz factory.[27] The leaf measures 32 by 23.5 centimeters, with, again, a total span of 19.4

centimeters. The paper is somewhat thick and grayish in color. The ink is dark brown.

The First Edition

The original edition of *Schwanengesang* was advertised for sale 4 May 1829 by Tobias Haslinger (1787–1842), reputed to have been the best music publisher of his time. Contemporary reviews of Schubert's music issued by Haslinger invariably refer to the quality of the engraver's work.[28] It may be remarked in passing that during his final illness the composer corrected proofs of part 2 of *Winterreise* as his last professional activity.[29] Schubert died on 19 November 1828. Less than a month later Haslinger became the first publisher to purchase music from the young composer's *Nachlass* (his estate). On 17 December he made a down payment for the fourteen songs that were to become *Schwanengesang*. The next day Haslinger wrote a letter to the official publication *Wiener Zeitung,* announcing the purchase and his intent to publish the songs as a group. The letter was printed by the periodical on 20 December. In January 1829 the energetic publisher announced details of the publication and called for a subscription to the initial printing with the inducement of an ornamented flyleaf with the subscriber's name. In March he advertised again and changed some details; among these changes was a higher price.[30]

To better understand the reasons for the excellence of the first edition, it may prove useful to review some details of the publisher's early life. Haslinger, born in Upper Austria, was a boy chorister in Linz, studied several instruments, and in addition to working in book and music stores, he composed music himself.[31] Not long after moving to Vienna in 1810, he joined the firm of S. A. Steiner, where he became a partner in 1815. From 1819 to 1826 he is reported to have devoted considerable effort to improving the quality of music printing, and in 1826 he became the principal owner of the firm, now renamed Tobias Haslinger. Earlier the firm of Steiner (and Haslinger) had become especially interested in the music of Beethoven and had published the first editions of a substantial number of the older composer's later works (Opp. 90–101, 112–118, 136–138, and several others). Following Beethoven's death in 1827, Haslinger began issuing a complete edition of Beethoven's music, a fact that could hardly have escaped Schubert's attention.[32] It is of particular interest to us that during the year he took over the Steiner firm, 1826, Haslinger had begun to publish recently written music by the young Viennese composer. And he continued to publish more works by Schubert than any other publisher until Schubert's death in 1828.[33]

Like the autograph, the copy of the first edition of *Schwanengesang* reproduced in this volume belongs to the Morgan Library (PMC 110). It is an exceptionally well-preserved lithograph in oblong format and two volumes, each with its original light-blue cover of a thick, porous paper. Each volume has a white, oblong label (16.7 by 11 centimeters) pasted to the front cover, on which the title is hyphenated. The paper used for the body of the publication is of high quality, showing remarkably little discoloration today. No doubt the rag content is quite high, if not 100 percent. The size of the paper and cover is 33.5 by 26.3 centimeters, slightly larger than that of the autograph.

An oval stamp on the title page of volume 1 indicates that the copy was once in the possession of J. G. Assmayer of Vienna, probably a book or music dealer. There is also a penciled price, "2 vols. $85.00," in the upper right-hand corner of the front flyleaf (recto) of volume 1.[34] The name "Julie Asten / April 1863" is written boldly with ink in the lower right-hand quadrant of the front cover of the second volume. On the otherwise blank verso of the title page of volume 1 there is a penciled entry reading "421.5 / S385," suggesting a library call number.[35]

Flyleaves, absent from volume 2, were inserted in volume 1 to accomodate the symbolically mournful decorative vignette (setting sun, weeping willow tree, and swan) printed on the page reserved for the name of the subscriber to the first edition. When this is present, and it is not in the copy used for the current edition, it occupies the recto of the front flyleaf. A copy of the vignette, without subscriber's name, appears at the conclusion of these introductory remarks. According to Deutsch, 158 subscribers ordered 180 copies.[36] As Haslinger suggested in his announcement of January 1929, the list of subscribers would "appear as a survey of Schubert's admirer's and friends, indeed in a way represent a list of the mourners' names."[37]

As a glance at the reprint in this volume will indicate, the collection was printed so that the songs could be sold separately. Each has a full title page on the recto of its initial folio. The music begins on the verso, with the title repeated at the top and the poet's name added. If the final page of a song is printed on the recto of a folio, the verso is blank. Haslinger assigned the plate number 5370 to the two title pages. These are identical except that the "Ite" (erste) "Abtheilung" was altered by pen and ink to "IIte" (zweite) for volume 2. Additionally, each of the fourteen songs has its own plate number (T. H. 5371–5384).

The publication has some interesting musical features. Unlike the *Neue Schubert-Ausgabe* of our day, Haslinger never follows a crescendo hairpin with an accent. Rather, he consistently prints the crescendo-decrescendo hairpins to be seen in Schubert's autographs. This interpretation by a responsible publisher who was himself a musician and composer, who was a contemporary of Schubert's, and who spent most of his adult life in Vienna, should be of particular interest to instrumentalists and singers today. A somewhat archaic feature of the edition, but one that also reflects the autograph, is the frequent placement of whole notes or dotted halves of triple meter in the middle of the measure rather than at the beginning.

Also noteworthy is the publisher's decision to print every strophe of "Frühlingsehnsucht" and "Ständchen" separately. As the autograph indicates, Schubert wrote out the music once for the stanzas of text treated strophically in both songs. Finally,

Haslinger's interpretation of an important correction on the last note of m. 39 of "Frühlingssehnsucht" is of interest. Unlike all other printed editions to the present day, he reads the change as *f′* to *e flat′* rather than the reverse. As almost always with Schubert's alterations, neither version is unmusical.

Unlike his great contemporary Beethoven, Schubert did not provide many clues to his compositional habits, or to his musical thinking. Although his output was large and many of his manuscripts are extant, it seems clear that a good number, perhaps the majority, of his compositional decisions were never written down. Certainly he did not leave a vast paper trail, as did Beethoven. There are relatively few letters or diary entries by Schubert, no conversation books—the younger composer was never deaf—and although a fair number of sketches are extant, that number does not come close to matching the number of sketches by Beethoven. Moreover, Schubert never left any formal sketch books, as Beethoven did. We are, therefore, fortunate in having the *Schwanengesang* sources. Here there are a number of different types of sketches, and although the autograph was clean enough to serve as the *Stichvorlage* for the first edition, there are enough corrections to provide clues to the way Schubert worked. Individuals who compare their own readings of the corrections with those suggested here, or with those reported in the "Quellen und Lesarten" of the *Neue Schubert-Ausgabe* (series 4, vol. 14b), will undoubtedly derive pleasure from their time spent with Schubert's attractively written autograph and sketches. In addition, they will gain insights into the composer's approach to composition that are available in no other way.

NOTES

1. The publication was announced as forthcoming in the *Wiener Zeitung* of 28 December 1828 and advertised for sale on 4 May 1829. *Franz Schubert: Thematisches Verzeichnis seiner Werke in chronologische Folge von Otto Erich Deutsch*, ed. W. Aderhold et al. (Kassel, 1978), 616–617. A facsimile edition of the seven Rellstab songs was published in Leipzig in 1941, and Walther Dürr edited a facsimile in slightly reduced size of the combined Rellstab and Heine songs as *Franz Schubert 'Schwanengesang,' 13 Lieder nach Gedichten von Rellstab und Heine* (Hildes-heim, 1978). The first page of "Die Taubenpost" was reproduced in Pierpont Morgan Library, *The Mary Flagler Cary Music Collection* (New York, [1970]). Of the sketches, only the manuscript of "Die Taubenpost" has been reproduced, in Ju. Chochlov, *O poslednem periode tvorčestva Suberta* (Moscow, 1968), and the first page appears in *Franz Schubert: Austellung der Wiener Stadt- und Landesbibliothek zum 150. Todestag des Komponist* (Vienna, 1978), both reduced in size. There has also been a reprint of the first edition in pocket format (Vienna, n.d.).

2. For biographical information about the three *Schwanengesang* poets, particularly with reference to Schubert, see chapter 2 of Martin Chusid, ed., *A Companion to Schubert's 'Schwanengesang'* (New Haven, 2000).

3. See Otto Erich Deutsch, *Schubert Reader* (New York, 1947), 844.

4. Robert Winter, "Paper Studies and the Future of Schubert Research," in *Schubert Studies*, ed. Eva Badura-Skoda and Peter Branscombe (Cambridge, England, 1982), 247. Earlier in the article, on a table of Schubert's music paper dating from 1823 to his death, he describes two batches of paper from Welhartitz used between June 1827 and October 1828 as "unclear watermark" and "barely visible watermark" (p. 222). It is also noteworthy that no watermarks are now visible on the sketch pages in Vienna (for "Liebesbotschaft" and "Frühlingssehnsucht" at the library of the Gesellschaft der Musikfreunde and for "Die Taubenpost" at the Vienna City Library), which are also identified by Winter as written on Welhartitz paper (p. 254). I am indebted to my colleagues Walther Dürr and Walburga Litschauer for this information. Some minor corrections may be made to Winter's pathbreaking study. On the table mentioned above, the final item on p. 222 lists thirty leaves of Winter's paper type VIId. But his discussion on pp. 253 and 254 indicates a total of seventy-one leaves. His calculations seem to omit the forty leaves belonging to the E-flat Mass. Further, on p. 253 the heading "Undated Works on Type VIId" is omitted from the compositions he lists as Nos. 3–8. On p. 254 the words "Sketches for" are missing from No. 4, "Songs, 'Lebensmut,' 'Liebesbotschaft' and 'Frühlingssehnsucht,'" and from No. 8, "Song, 'Die Taubenpost.'"

5. Winter, "Paper Studies," paper type VIII, 275.

6. Some of these lapses are listed in the section "Quellen und Lesarten" of Walther Dürr's edition of the songs of *Schwanengesang* in the *Neue Schubert-Ausgabe* (Kassel, 1988), series IV, vol. 14b. Many others will be found in the mimeographed *Kritische Bericht* to that volume prepared by the editor, Dürr, and deposited at major libraries around the world. In the United States

the depository is the Library of Congress; in England it is the British Library.

7. Dürr, "Quellen und Lesarten," *Neue Schubert-Ausgabe*, series IV, vol. 14b, 328.

8. Those who hold this view include Eusebius Mandyczewski, editor of *Schwanengesang* in the old complete edition (Leipzig, 1895, series 20, part 5) and Walther Dürr of the new (Kassel, 1988, series IV, vol. 14a) as well as Max Friedlaender, who edited the old Peters edition of the Schubert Lieder (Leipzig, n.d.). The first edition, however, assumed the change to have been from the *f″* to the *e flat″*. See the reprint in this volume and the facsimile of the autograph itself. In the parallel situation of the final, minor strophe, Schubert quite clearly changed from *e flat* to *f flat″*, otherwise why not delete the flat sign? See also the discussion below.

9. Measure numbering as in the *Neue Schubert-Ausgabe*. In many editions the measure number is 84 because the texts of all four strophes in B-flat major are set with the same music, as in Schubert's autograph.

10. The reading of the original sonority of m. 108 in the "Quellen und Lesarten" of the *Neue Schubert-Ausgabe*, series IV, vol. 14b, 330, is not possible: "Keyboard upper part: Triplet eighths originally with *c sharp′*; Keyboard lower part: originally with halves *c + e + g*." Schubert's ear would never have tolerated the simultaneous cross relation (*c natural + c sharp′*) without considerably better linear justification than here. Clearly the *c natural* was a substitute for the *e*, which was also the lowest pitch in m. 107, and was added after the composer had deleted the *c sharps′* from the right hand.

11. See chapter 3 of *A Companion to Schubert's 'Schwanengesang,'* where Edward Cone indicates the importance of the movement 5–flat 6–5 in "Kriegers Ahnung." In chapter 4 of that volume, I suggest that this same motion may be important for several of the other Rellstab songs as well, including "In der Ferne."

12. See Edward Cone, chapter 3 in *A Companion to Schubert's 'Schwanengesang,'* for the importance of this motive as a recurring figure throughout the Heine songs, and chapter 4 in the same volume for my discus-

sion of the relationship of this figure to the opening theme of the Allegro in Beethoven's last piano sonata, Op. 111.

13. See chapter 4 of *A Companion to Schubert's 'Schwanengesang,'* especially the section on "Kriegers Ahnung," for a discussion of Schubert's use of the major and minor modes in relation to the meaning of his song texts.

14. See the discussion of these songs in ibid.

15. See Mandyczewski's remarks on "Frühlingssehnsucht" in the volume of critical commentary to the old complete edition (Leipzig, 1897).

16. Not to be confused with Schubert's setting of the poem "Lebensmut" by Ernst Schulze (D. 883, March 1826). Interestingly enough, the two songs are in the same key, B-flat major, and both make use of an energetic rhythmic pattern consisting of an eighth note and two sixteenths. Although the Rellstab song has no tempo indication, the designation for the Schulze Lied, "Ziemlich geschwind, doch kräftig," would seem to be appropriate for the later composition as well. Both songs are to be found in the *Neue Schubert-Ausgabe*, series IV, the Schulze song in vol. 14a, the Rellstab "fragment" in 14b. They also appear in the old complete edition, edited by Mandyczewski, series 20, part 5, nos. 497 and 602.

17. The song is recorded in this fashion by Dietrich Fischer-Dieskau in his recording of most of Schubert's Lieder for Deutsche Grammophon. See also the similarly structured song by Schubert "Herbst" (D. 945), also on a text by Rellstab.

18. For the complete poem see *A Companion to Schubert's 'Schwanengesang,'* chapter 4.

19. See *Franz Schubert Thematisches Verzeichnis*, 616. The owner was a Herr Oppenheim of Budapest.

20. In this regard see the remarks about "Ständchen" by Edward Cone in chapter 3 of *A Companion to Schubert's 'Schwanengesang.'*

21. This phrase is used in Verdi studies, for example. See my discussion of the *Abozzo* in the "Introduction" to *Rigoletto*, vol. 17 in the new complete edition, *The Works of Giuseppe Verdi* (Chicago, Milan, 1983). See especially the separate volume of critical commentary,

5–9. In Wagner studies the term often used is "compositional draft."

22. All measure numbers in the discussions of "Die Taubenpost" and "Liebesbotschaft" refer to the final version of the song.

23. While discussing the broken chords of the harpist in "Wer sich der Einsamkeit ergibt," Dürr says, "Schubert loves to create a kind of stage-set in this way." "Schubert's Songs and their Poetry," in Badura-Skoda and Branscombe, *Schubert Studies*, 17.

24. Regarding Schubert's initial concentration on the poetry, see the beginning of chapter 6 in *A Companion to Schubert's 'Schwanengesang.'*

25. Information about physical characteristics was kindly provided by Walther Dürr and Walburga Litschauer.

26. Robert Winter, "Paper Studies," 254, where the paper is identified as Winter's type VII D. See also p. 247.

27. Ibid.

28. See Deutsch, *Schubert Reader*, 675 (Op. 78), 721 (Opp. 79–81), 727 (Op. 83), and 759 (*Winterreise*, part I).

29. Ibid., 821.

30. Ibid., 844.

31. Biographical details are primarily from Alexander Weinmann's articles in *Die Musik in Geschichte und Gegenwart* (Kassel, 1956) and *The New Grove Dictionary of Music and Musicians* (London, 1980).

32. The edition was never completed.

33. These included Opp. 77–83 and 89–91, as well as the male quartets without opus numbers, "Grab und Mond" and "Wein und Liebe." See Deutsch, *Schubert Reader*, 904.

34. Prices appear to have been erased from the upper-right-hand corners of the front covers of both volumes.

35. Near the bottom of the title page of volume I is another penciled number, "60971."

36. Deutsch, *Schubert Reader*, 884.

37. Ibid. Deutsch includes a selection from the list of subscribers. A complete list of subscribers may be found in the German edition, *Die Dokumente seines Lebens* (Kassel, 1964), 575–578

THE *Schwanengesang* AUTOGRAPH

D. 957 nos. 1–13 and D. 965A

Original at the Pierpont Morgan Library, New York

"Liebesbotschaft," braces 1–5: mm. 1–5, 6–10, 11–16, 17–21, 22–25   3

"Liebesbotschaft," braces 1–5: mm. 26–30, 31–35, 36–40, 41–44, 45–49

"Liebesbotschaft," braces 1–5: mm. 50–53, 54–58, 59–64, 65–70, 71–75   5

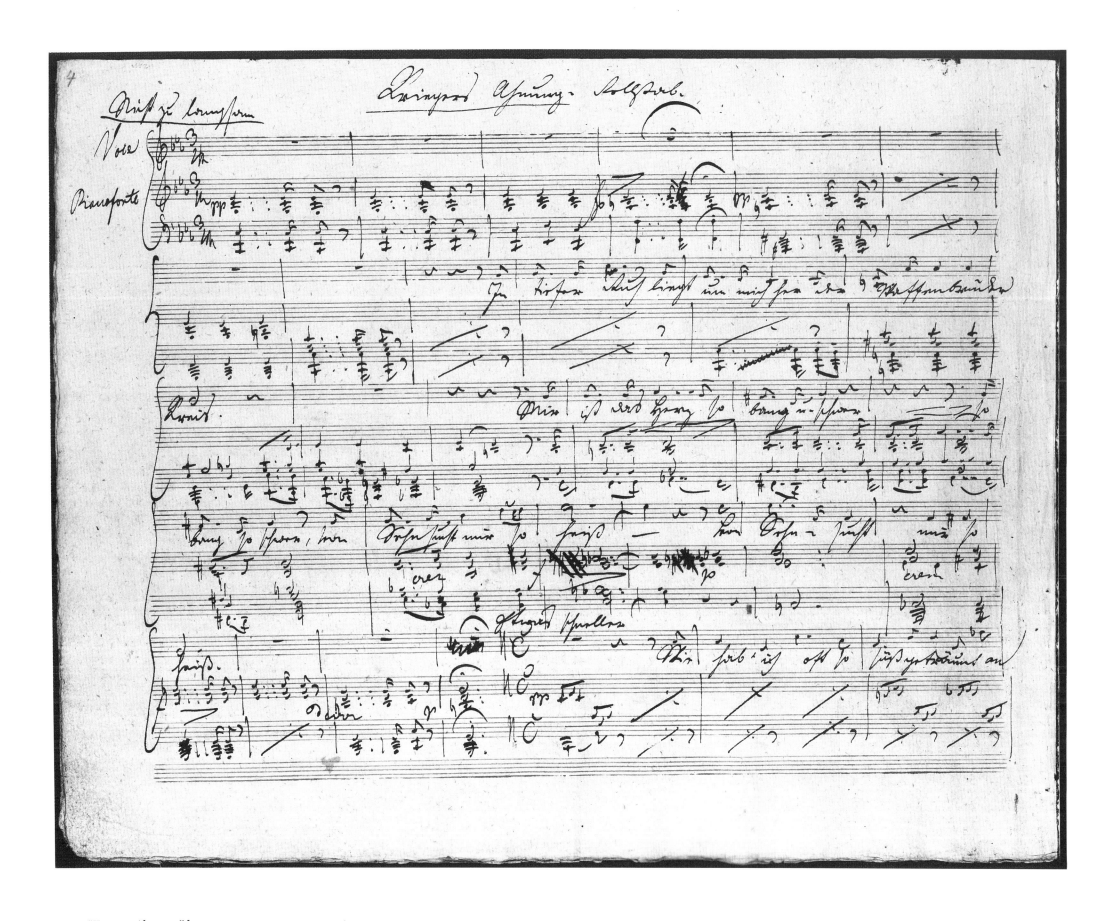

"Kriegers Ahnung," braces 1–5: mm. 1–6, 7–12, 13–18, 19–24, 25–31

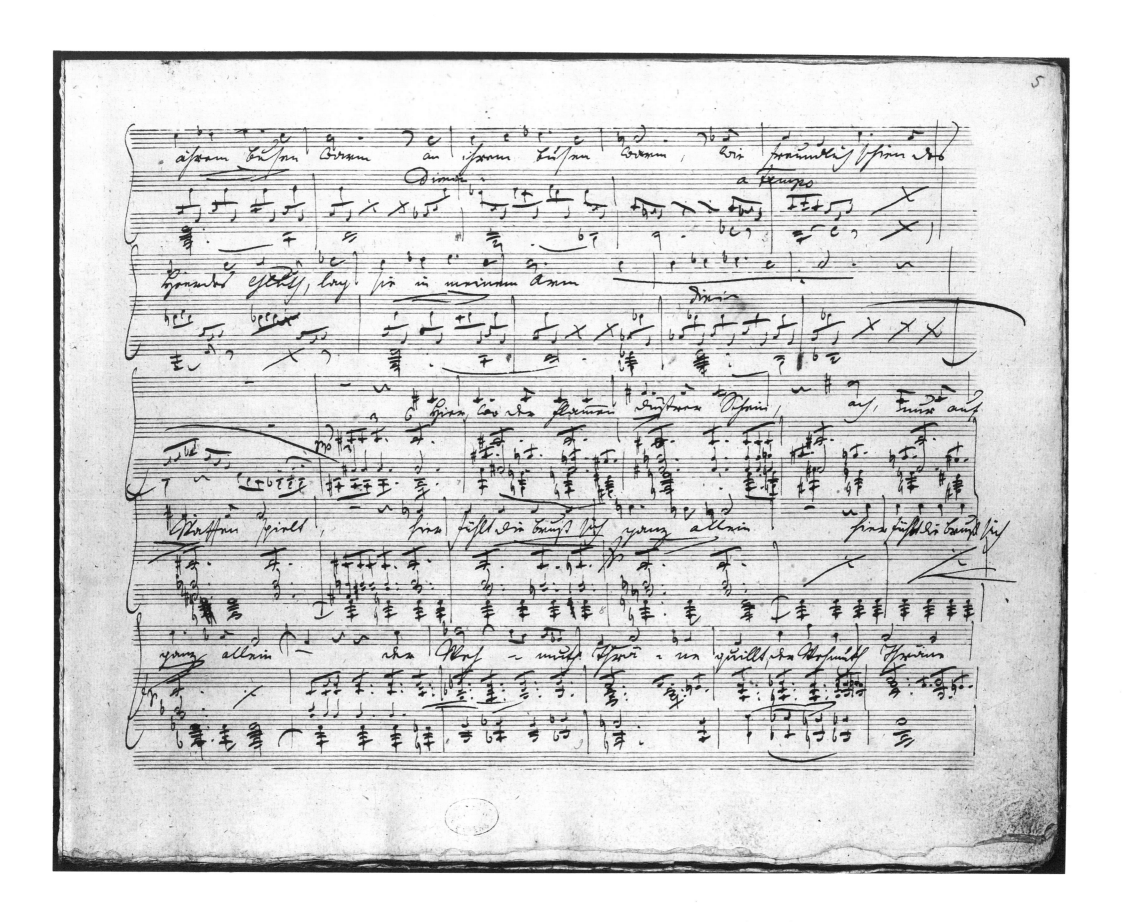

8   *"Kriegers Ahnung," braces 1–5: mm. 59–64, 65–70, 71–77, 78–85, 86–91*

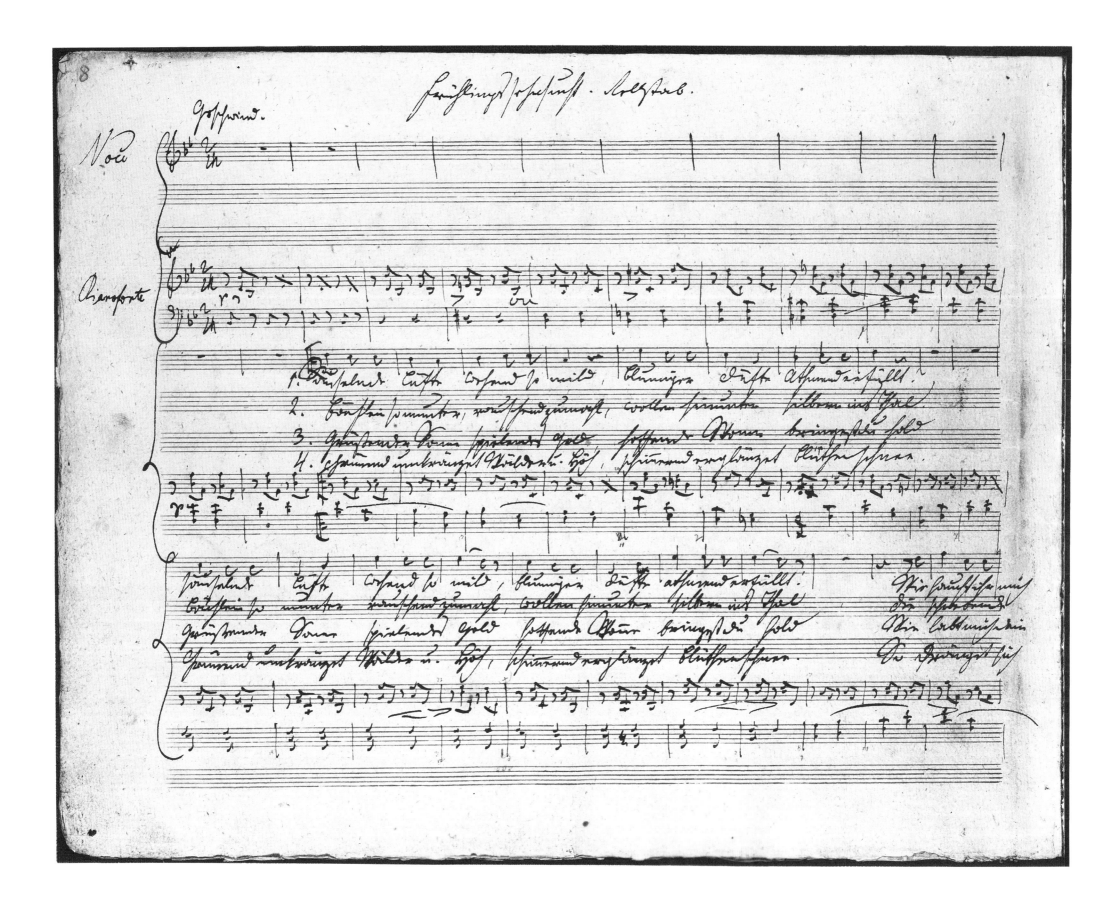

10   *"Frühlingssehnsucht," braces 1–3: mm. 1–10, 11–22, 23–33*

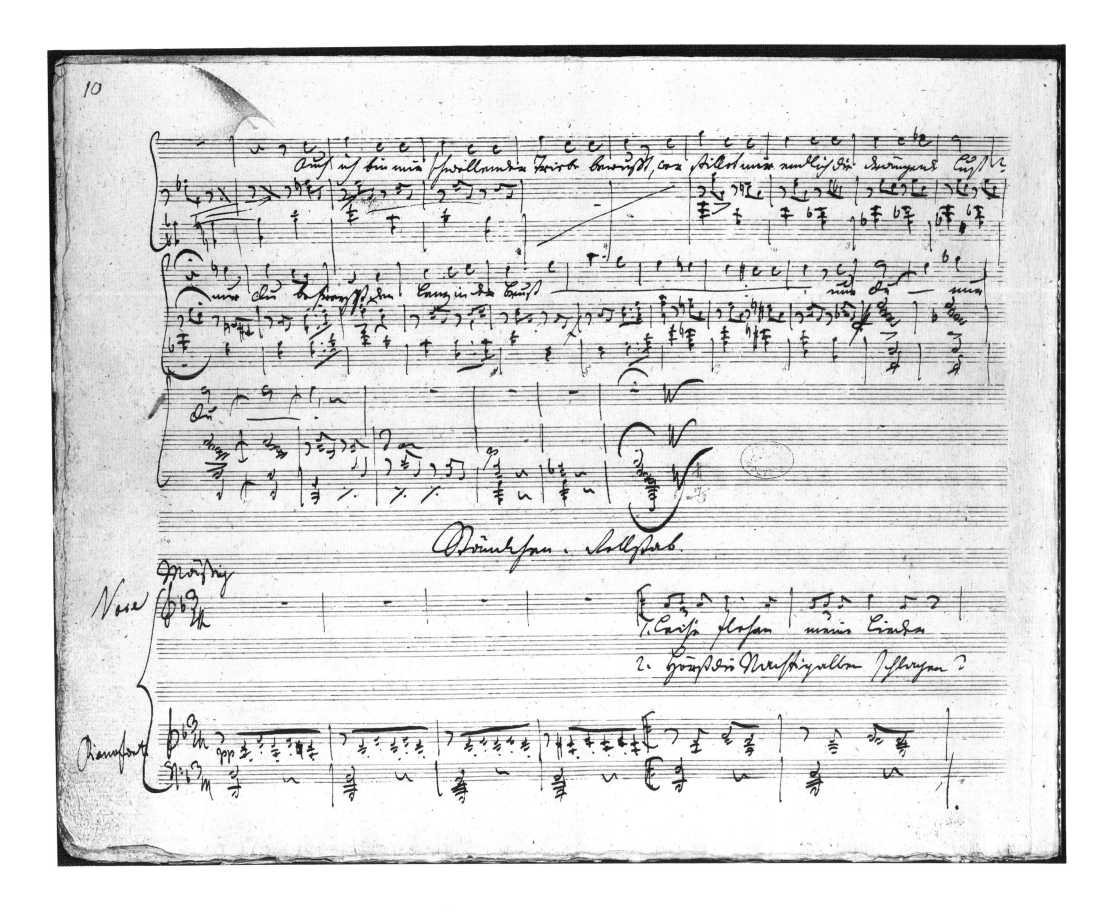

12   *"Frühlingssehnsucht," braces 1–3: mm. 76–85, 86–96, 97–103; "Ständchen," brace 4: mm. 1–6*

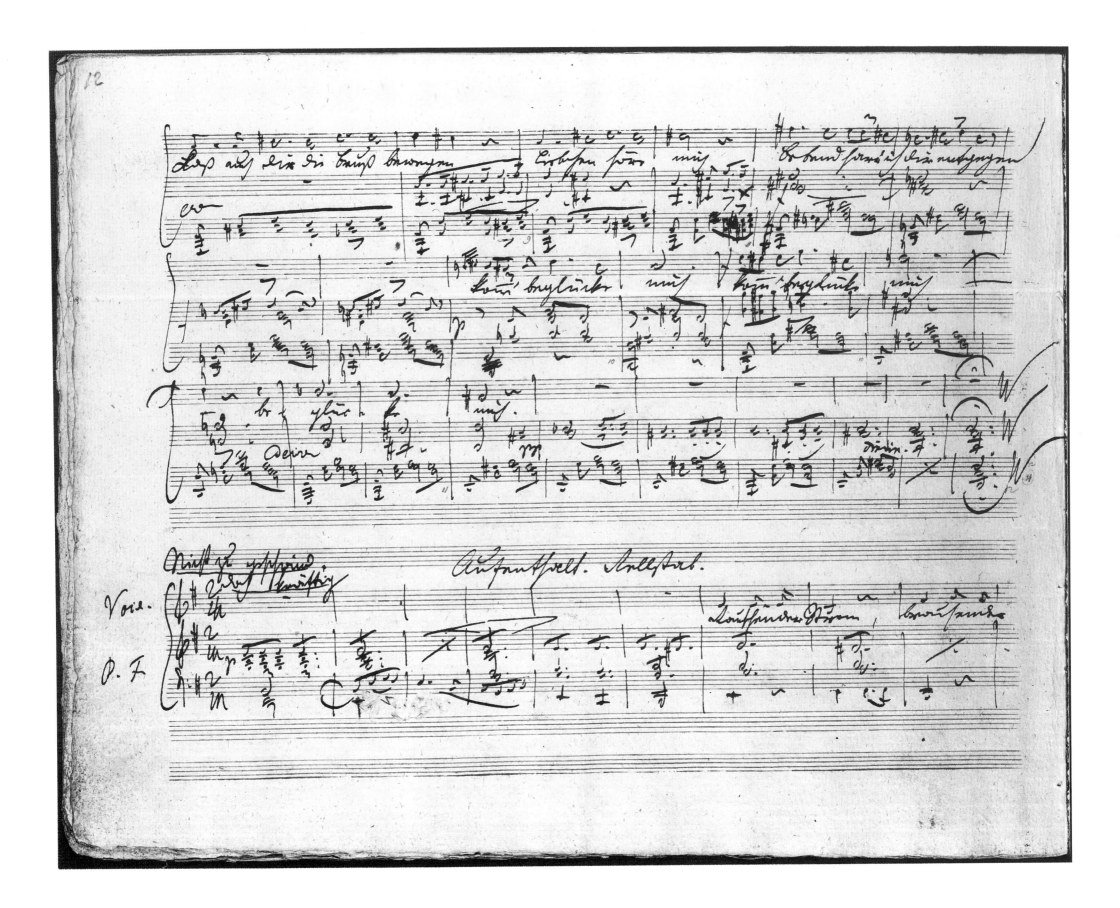

14   "Ständchen," braces 1–3: mm. 29–34, 35–40, 41–50; "Aufenthalt," brace 4: mm. 1–9

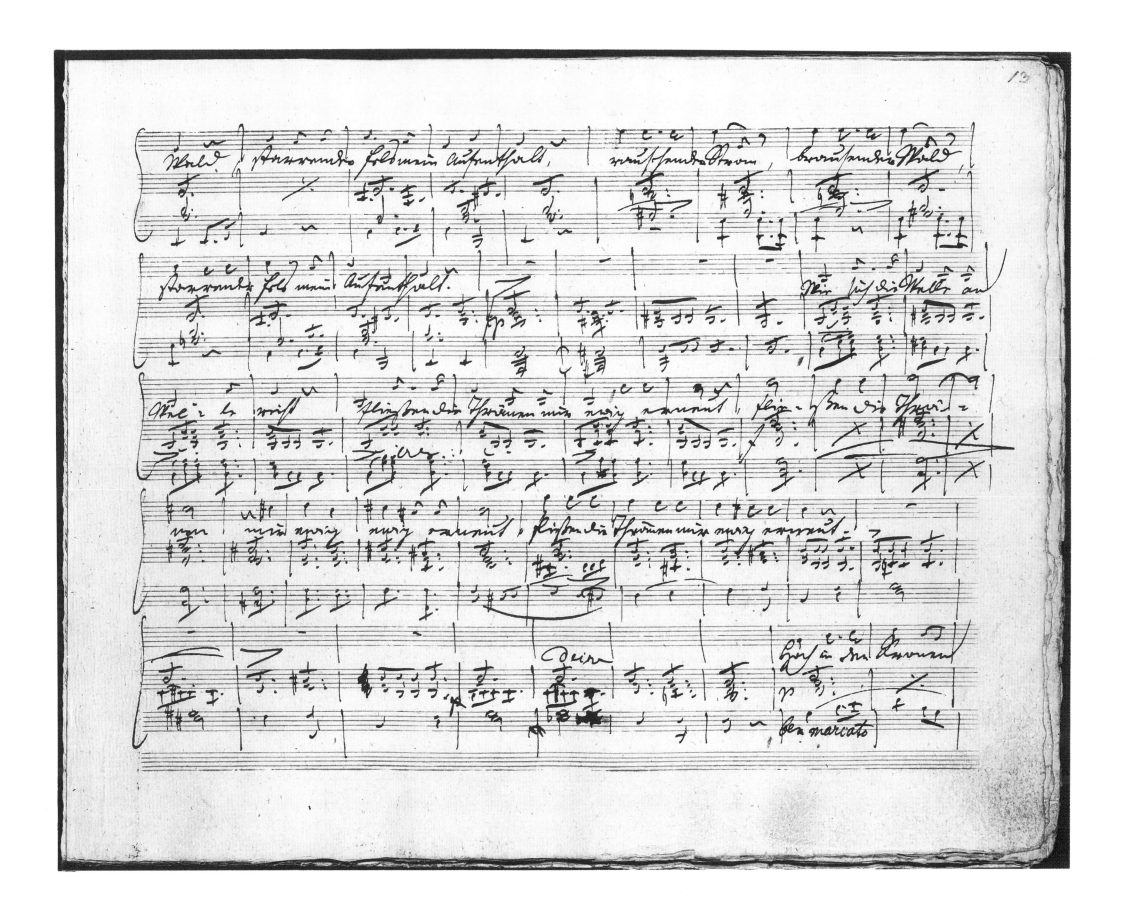

16   *"Aufenthalt," braces 1–5: mm. 58–66, 67–75, 76–84, 85–95, 96–106*

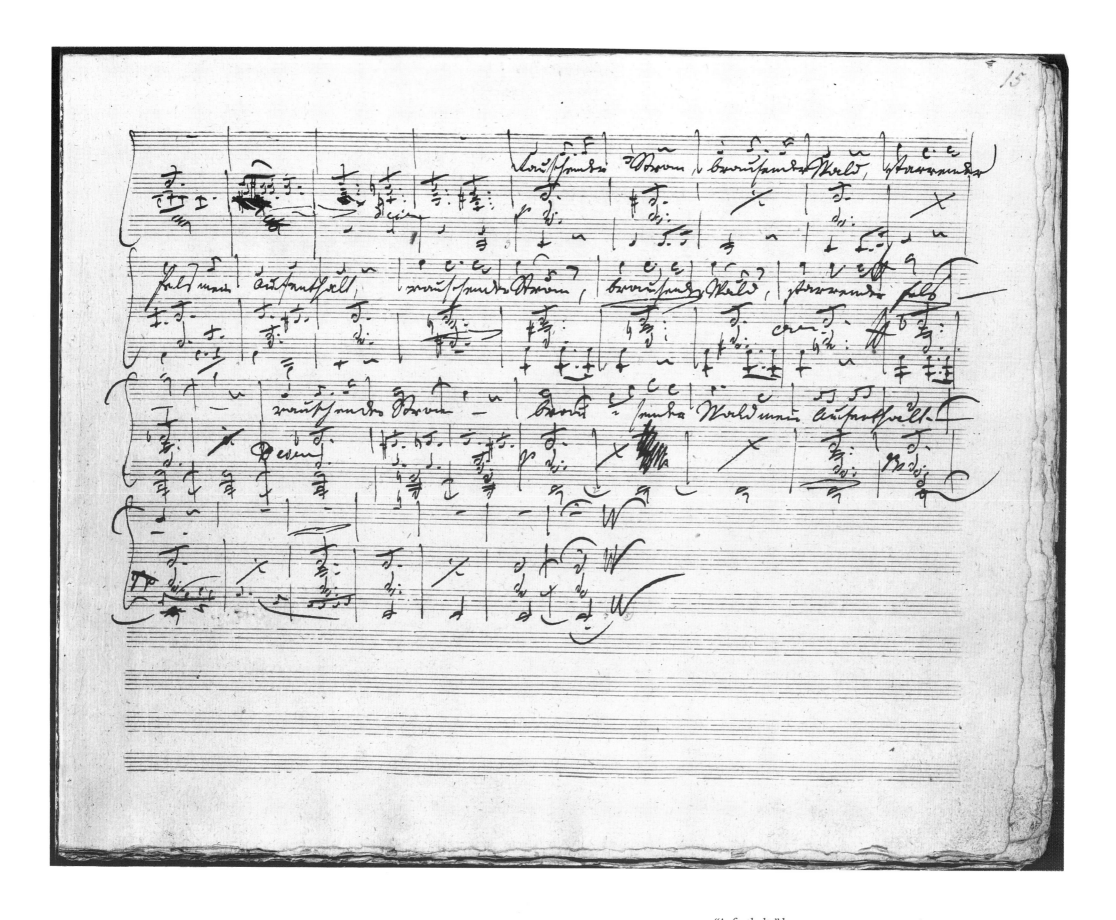

"Aufenthalt," braces 1–4: mm. 107–115, 116–124, 125–134, 135–141 17

18 *"In der Ferne,"* braces 1–5: mm. 1–9, 10–17, 18–25, 26–36, 37–44

"In der Ferne," braces 1–5: mm. 45–52, 53–62, 63–71, 72–81, 82–91 19

18

20   "In der Ferne," braces 1–3: mm. 92–102, 103–112, 113–117; "Abschied," brace 4: mm. 1–6

"Abschied," braces 1–5: mm. 7–12, 13–17, 18–21, 22–26, 27–34 21

"Abschied," braces 1–5: mm. 35–40, 41–45, 46–49, 50–55, 56–61

24   *"Abschied,"* braces 1–5: mm. 89–93, 94–98, 99–103, 104–109, 110–115

26 *"Abschied," braces 1–4: mm. 144–148, 149–153, 154–160, 161–167*

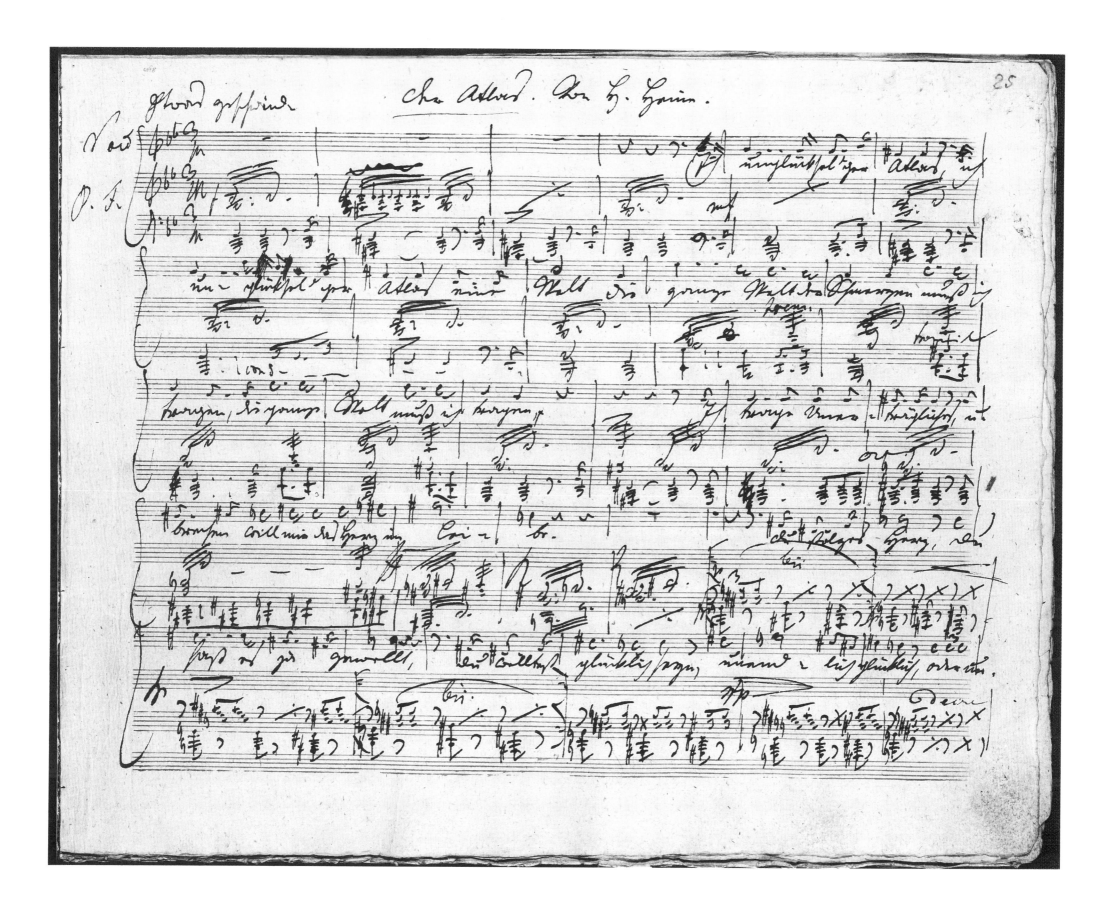

"Der Atlas," braces 1–5: mm. 1–6, 7–11, 12–17, 18–24, 25–30   27

"Der Atlas," braces 1–5: mm. 31–37, 38–43, 44–48, 49–54, 55–56

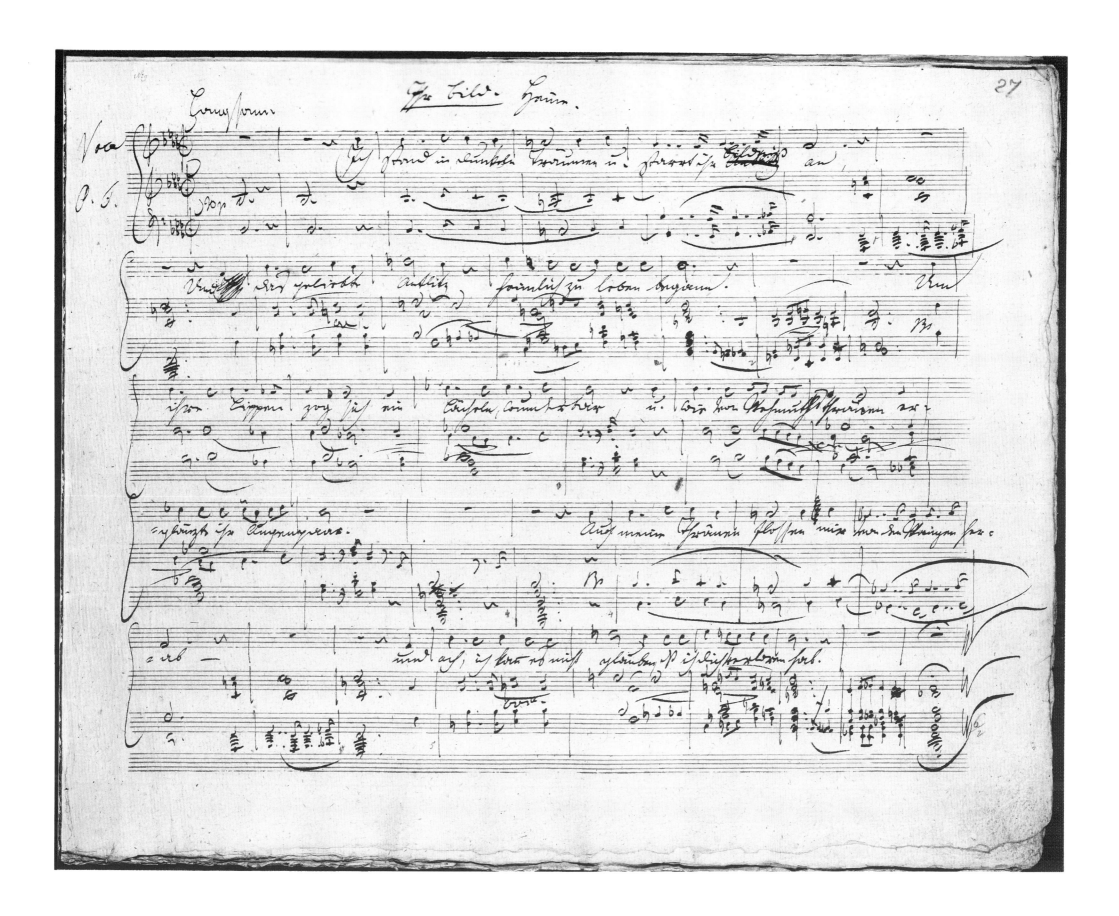

"Das Fischermädchen," braces 1–5: mm. 1–7, 8–14, 15–21, 22–29, 30–36

"Das Fischermädchen," braces 1–5: mm. 37–43, 44–51, 52–59, 60–67, 68–72   31

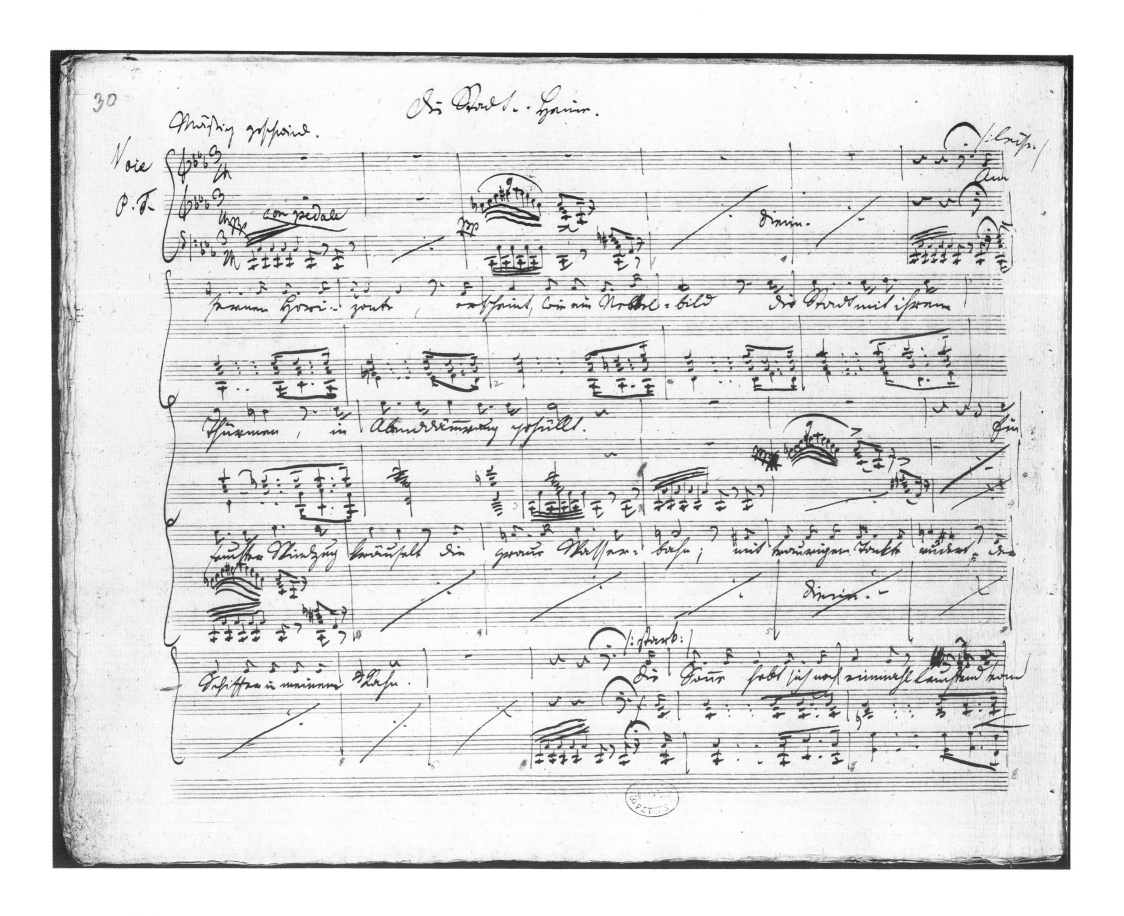

32   *"Die Stadt," braces 1–5: mm. 1–6, 7–11, 12–17, 18–23, 24–29*

31

34   *"Am Meer," braces 1–5: mm. 13–18, 19–23, 24–28, 29–34, 35–39*

34

"Der Doppelgänger," braces 1–5: mm. 28–35, 36–40, 41–47, 48–53, 54–63

"Die Taubenpost," braces 1–4: mm. 1–6, 7–12, 13–18, 19–24   37

"Die Taubenpost," braces 1–4: mm. 25–30, 31–35, 36–40, 41–46

"Die Taubenpost," braces 1–4: mm. 72–77, 78–84, 85–90, 91–98

THREE SKETCHES FOR *Schwanengesang*

"Liebesbotschaft"

D. 957 no. 1 · A Skeleton Score

Original at the Gesellschaft der Musikfreunde, Vienna

"Frühlingssehnsucht"

D. 957 no. 3 · A Preliminary Sketch Fragment

Original at the Gesellschaft der Musikfreunde, Vienna

"Die Taubenpost"

D. 965A · A Continuity Draft

Original at the Stadtbibliothek, Vienna

44   *"Liebesbotschaft," braces 2–5: mm. (6–12), (13–19), (20–25), (26–31)*

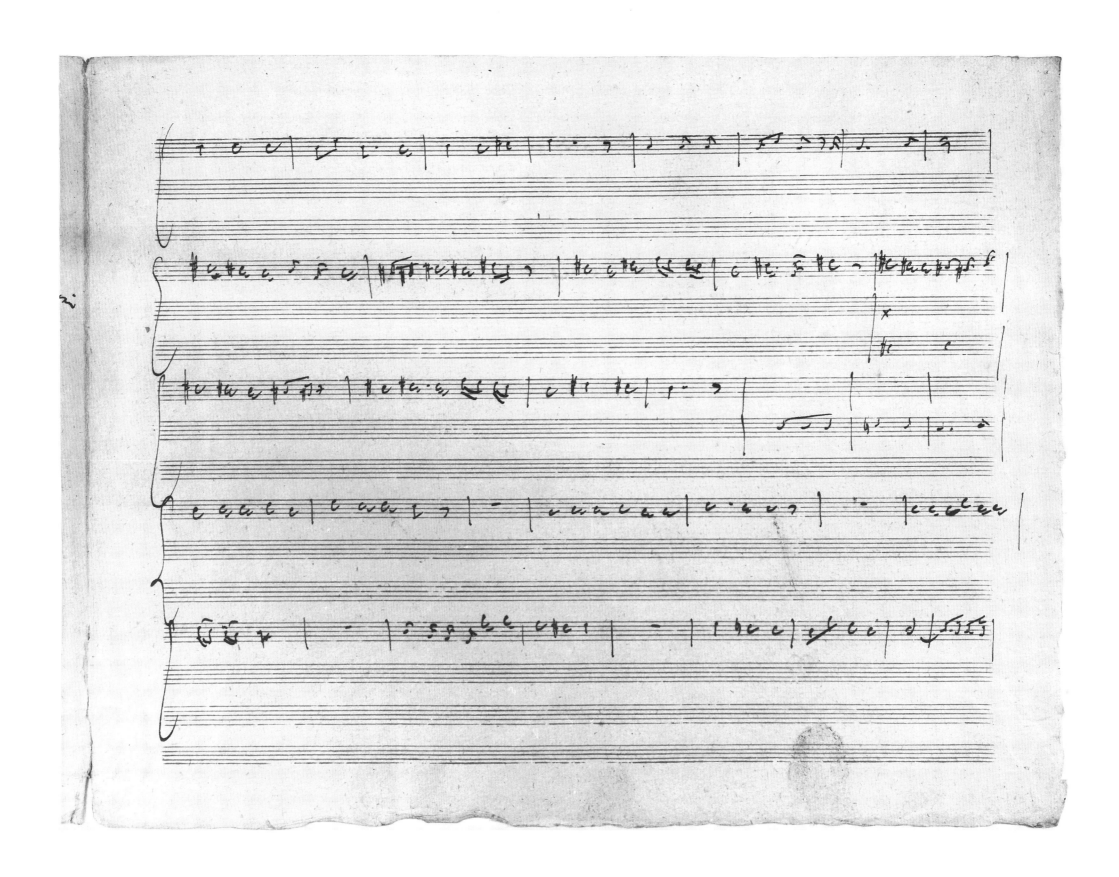

"Liebesbotschaft," braces 1–5: mm. (32–39), (40–44), (45–51), (52–58), (59–67)   45

46   *"Frühlingssehnsucht," title and braces 1–3: mm. 1–5, 6–10, 11*

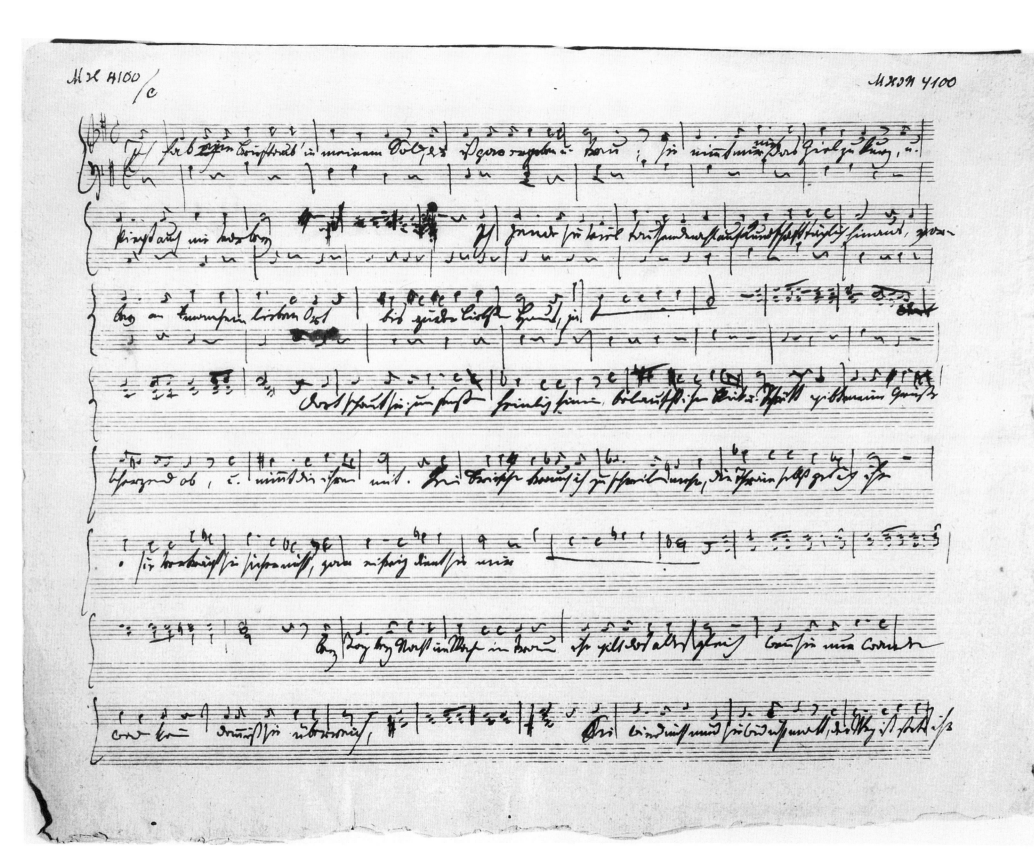

"Die Taubenpost," braces 1–8: mm. 1–6 (6–11), 7–14 (12–19), 15–22 (20–27), 23–29 (28–34), 30–36 (35–41), 37–44 (42–49), 45–51 (50–56), 52–59 (57–64)   47

"Die Taubenpost," braces 1–5: mm. 60–67 (65–71), 68–74 (72–75), 75–84 (76–85), 85–93 (86–94), 94–100 (95–101)

Schwanengesang THE FIRST EDITION

D. 957 nos. 1–13 and D. 965A

Reprinted from a copy at the Pierpont Morgan Library, New York

SCHWANEN-GESANG.

VON

Franz Schubert.

1te Abtheilung.

7.

WIEN, BEI TOBIAS HASLINGER.

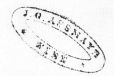

SCHWANENGESANG.

In Musik gesetzt

für eine Singstimme mit Begleitung des Pianoforte

von

Franz Schubert

LETZTES WERK.

Ite Abtheilung.

No. 5370. —— Eigenthum des Verlegers. —— Preis f 3 CM.

❋

Wien, bey Tobias Haslinger,
Musikverleger,
im Hause der ersten österr: Sparkasse
am Graben No 572.

INHALT.

———————— * ————————

T H 5371.

I.

Liebesbothschaft,

von

FRANZ SCHUBERT.

———— ✴ ————

(5371.)

Eigenthum u. Verlag von Tob. Haslinger in Wien.

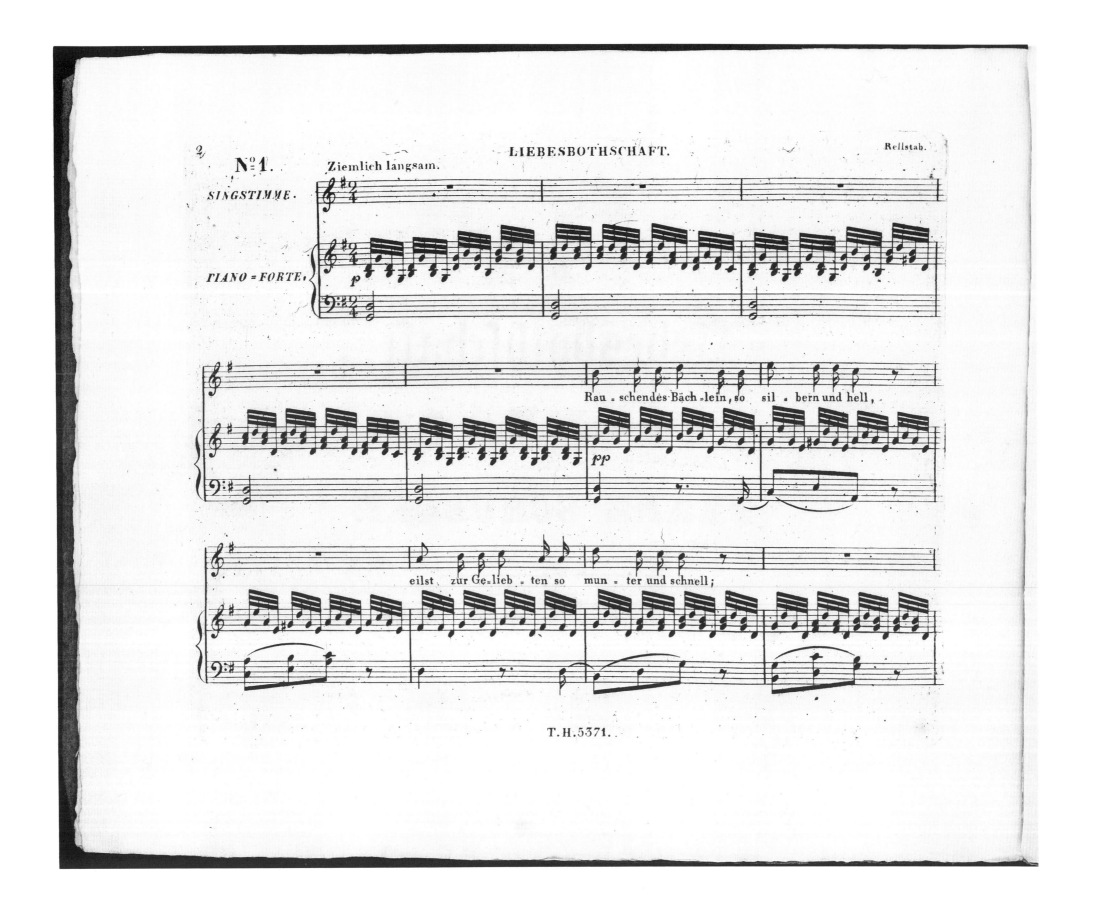

"Liebesbotschaft," braces 1–3: mm. 1–3, 4–7, 8–11

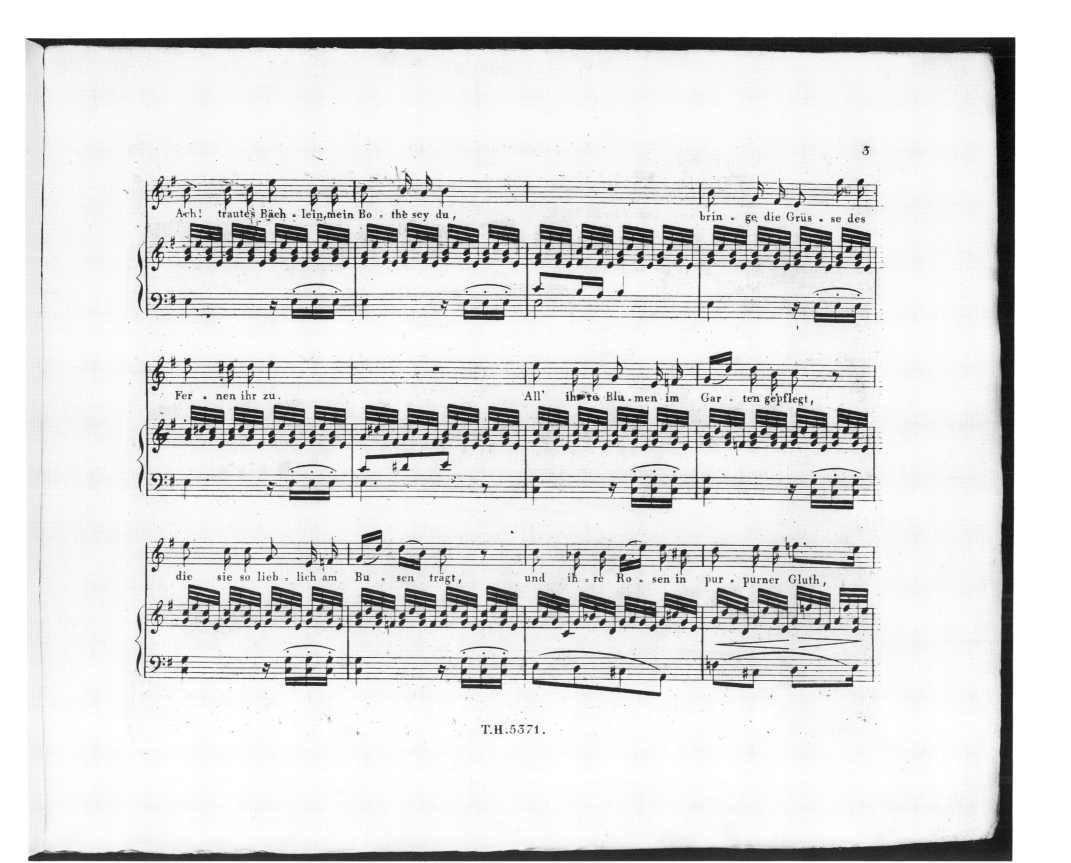

T.H.5371.

4

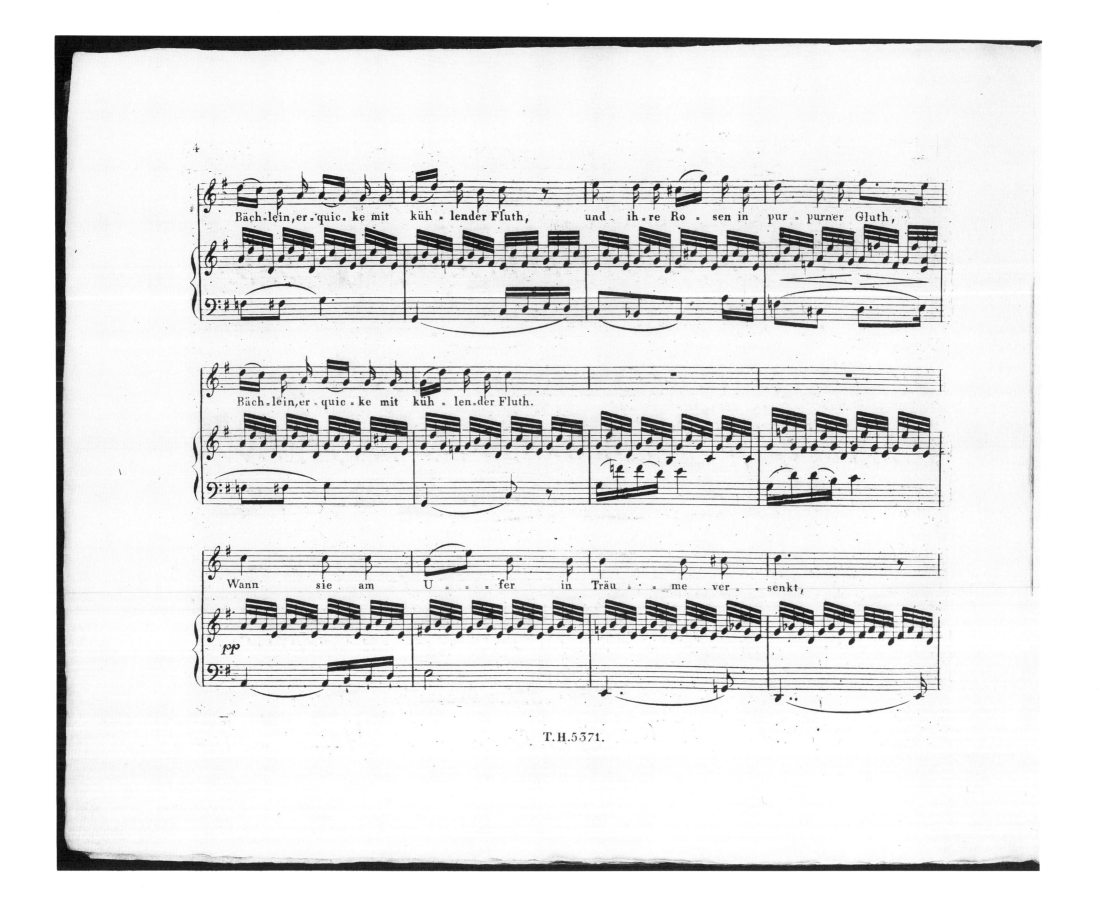

Bäch=lein, er=quic=ke mit küh=lender Fluth, und ih=re Ro=sen in pur=purner Gluth,

Bäch=lein, er=quic=ke mit küh=len=der Fluth.

Wann sie am U==fer in Träu==me ver==senkt,

pp

T.H.5371.

58   *"Liebesbotschaft," braces 1–3: mm. 24–27, 28–31, 32–35*

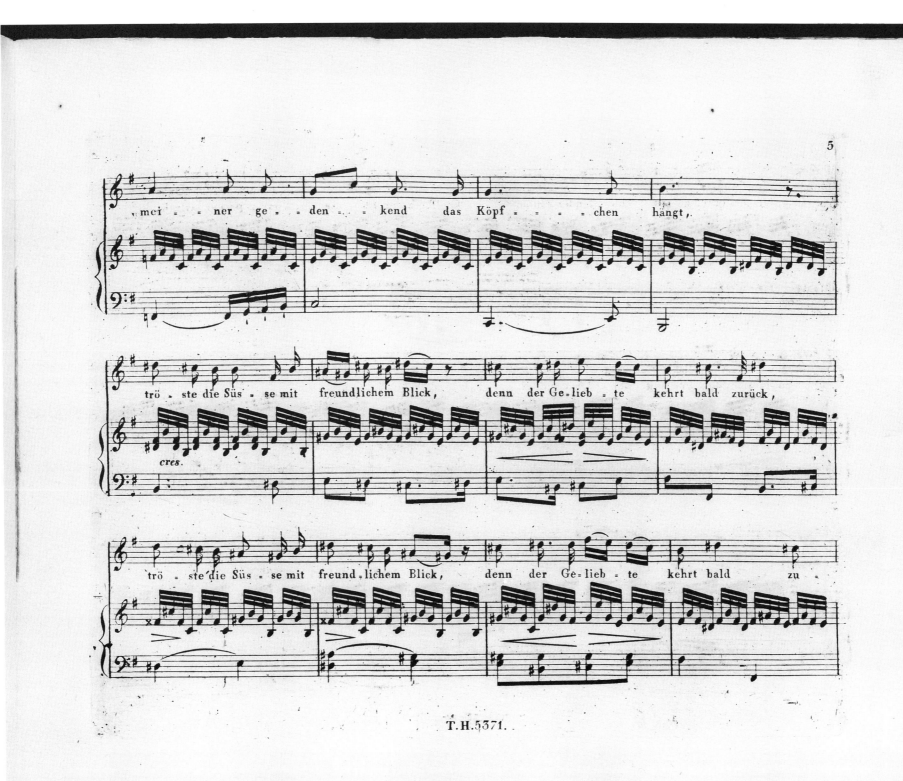

T.H.5371.

6

rück.

Neigt sich die Son = ne mit

decres.

pp

röth = lichem Schein,

wie = ge das Liebchen in   Schlummer ein,

rau = sche sie murmelnd in   süs = se Ruh,

flü = stre ihr Träu = me der Lie = be   zu,

T.H.5571.

60   "Liebesbotschaft," braces 1–3: mm. 48–52, 53–57, 58–62

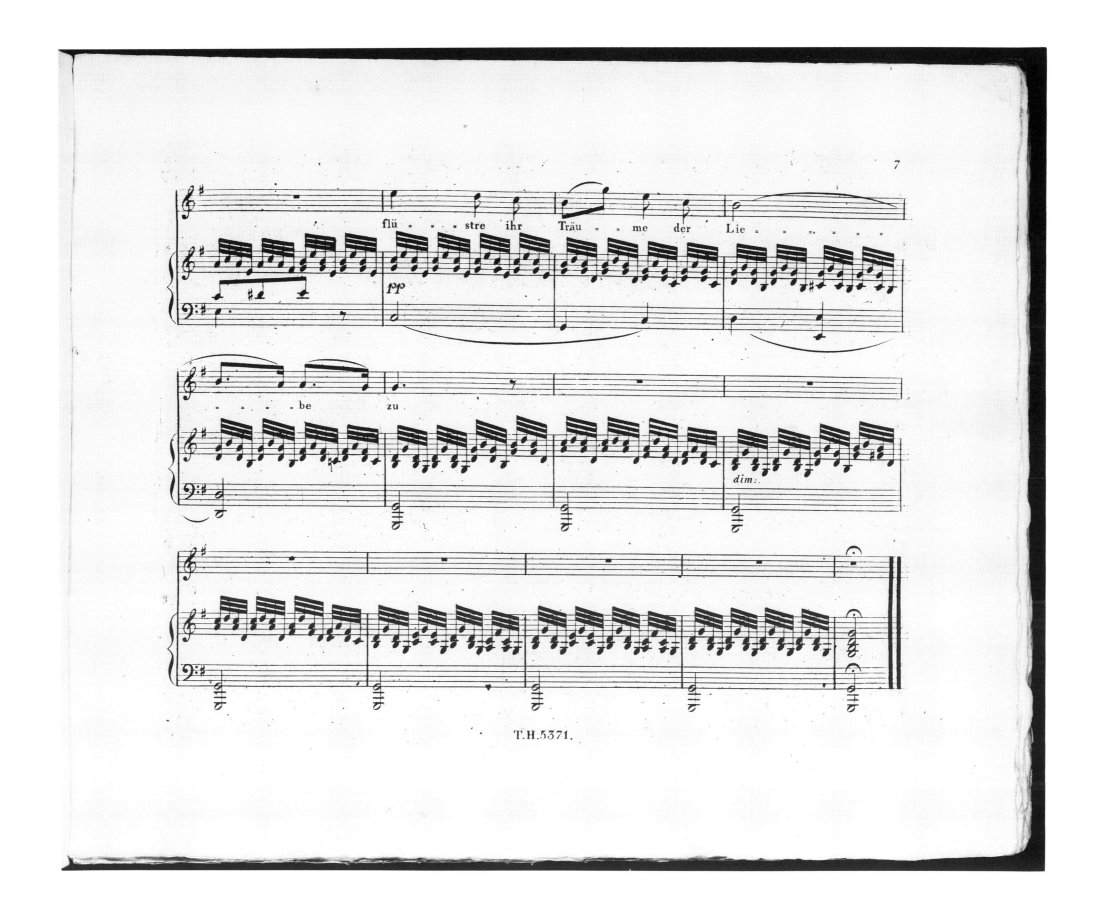

7

flü — — stre ihr Träu — — me der Lie

pp

— — — be zu

dim:

T.H.5371.

II.

Kriegers Ahnung,

von

FRANZ SCHUBERT.

———— * ————

(5372.)
Eigenthum u. Verlag von Tob. Haslinger in Wien.

"Kriegers Ahnung," braces 1–3: mm. 1–7, 8–15, 16–22

"Kriegers Ahnung," braces 1–3: mm. 41–45, 46–52, 53–59

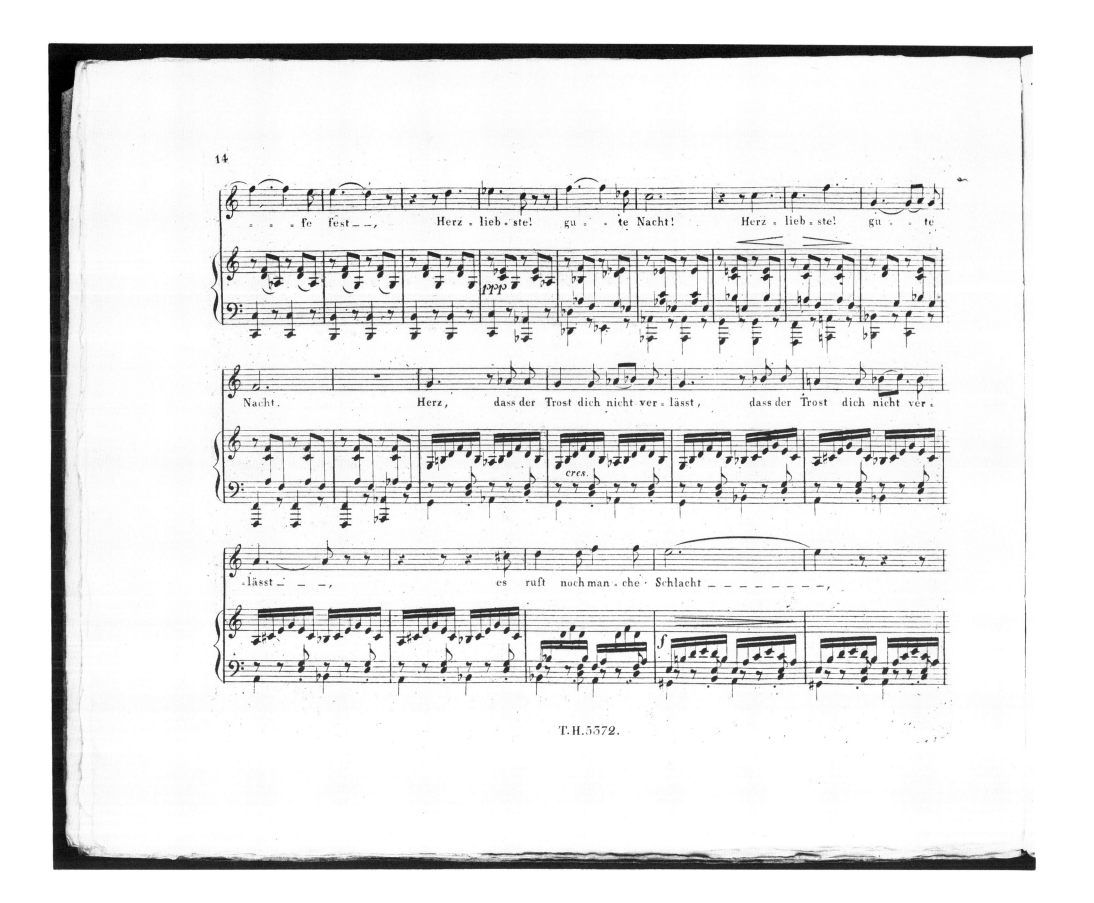

"Kriegers Ahnung," braces 1–3: mm. 78–86, 87–92, 93–97

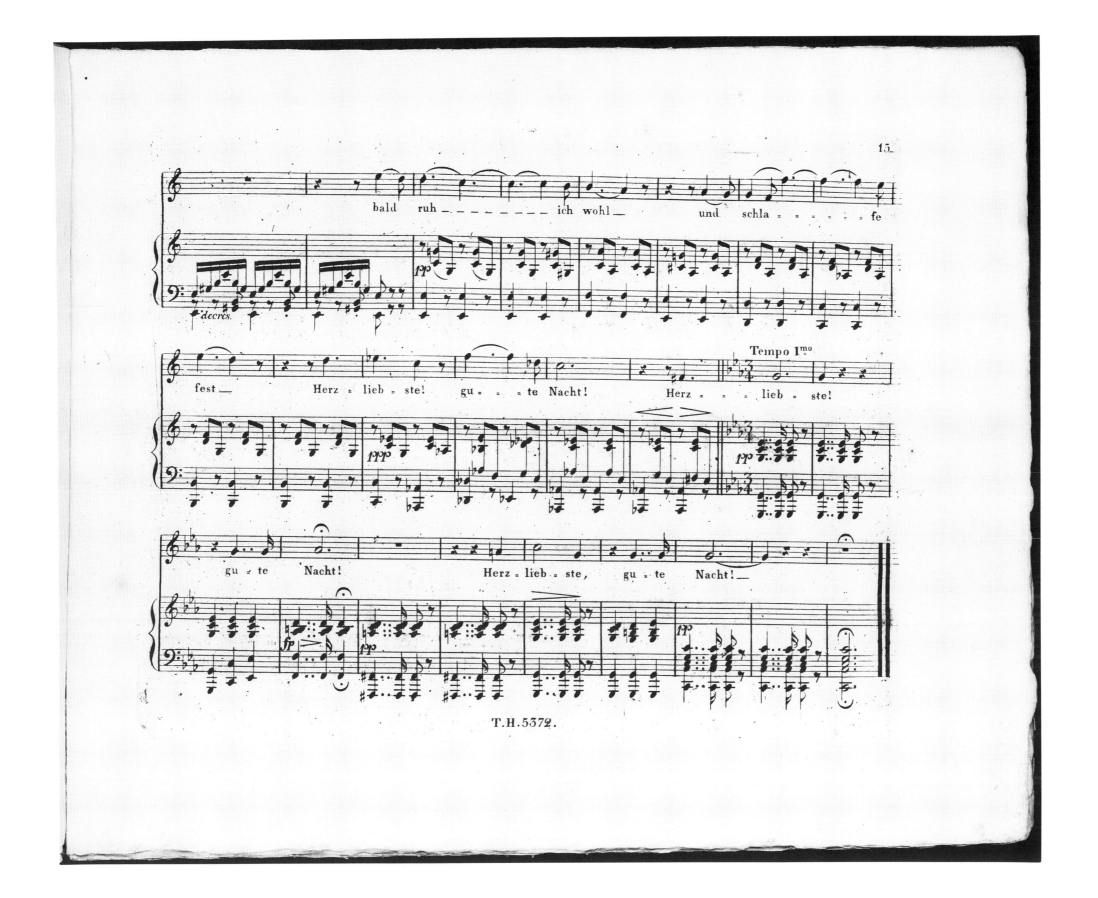

15.

III.

Frühlingssehnsucht,

von

FRANZ SCHUBERT.

———*———

(5373.)
Eigenthum u. Verlag von Tob. Haslinger in Wien.

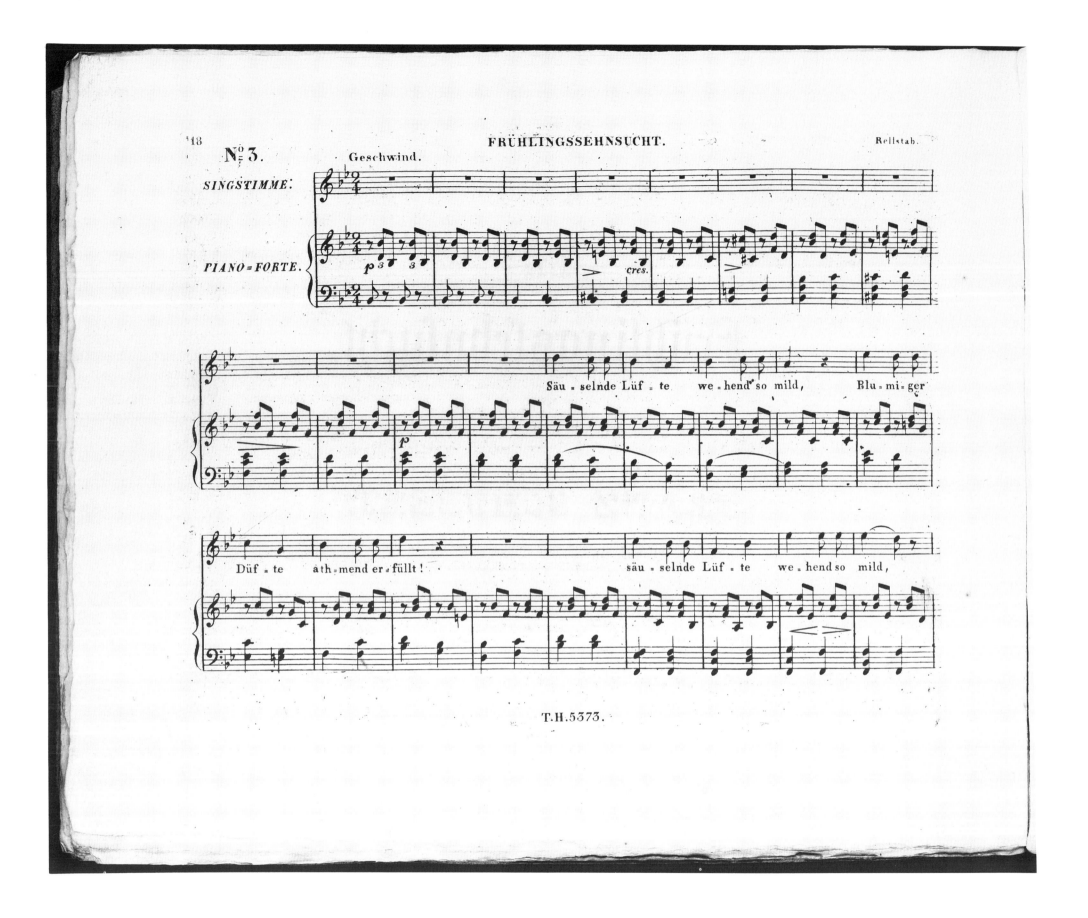

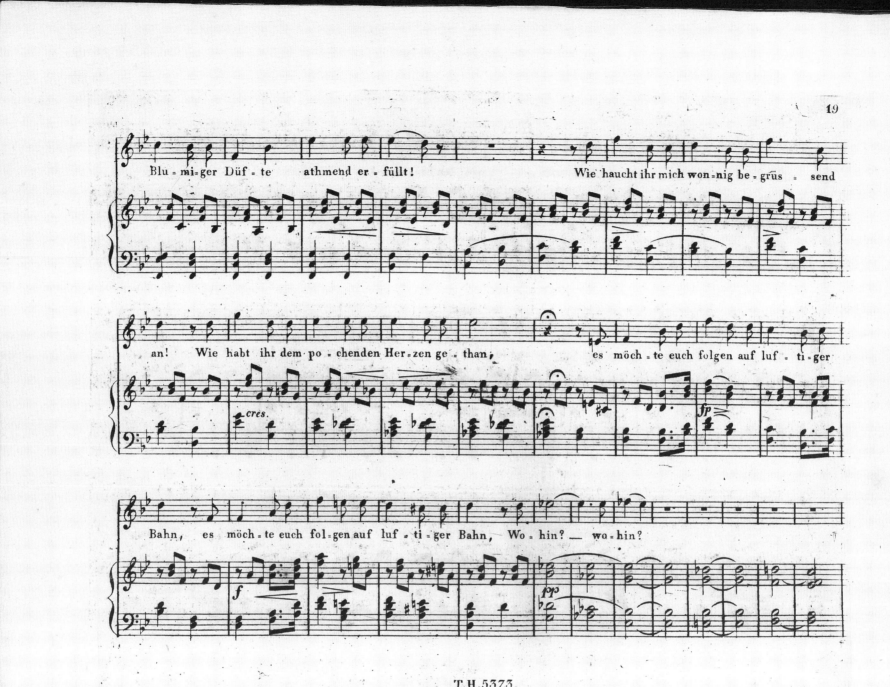

T.H.5373.

20

T. H. 5373.

74   *"Frühlingssehnsucht,"* braces 1–3: mm. 58–66, 67–75, 76–84

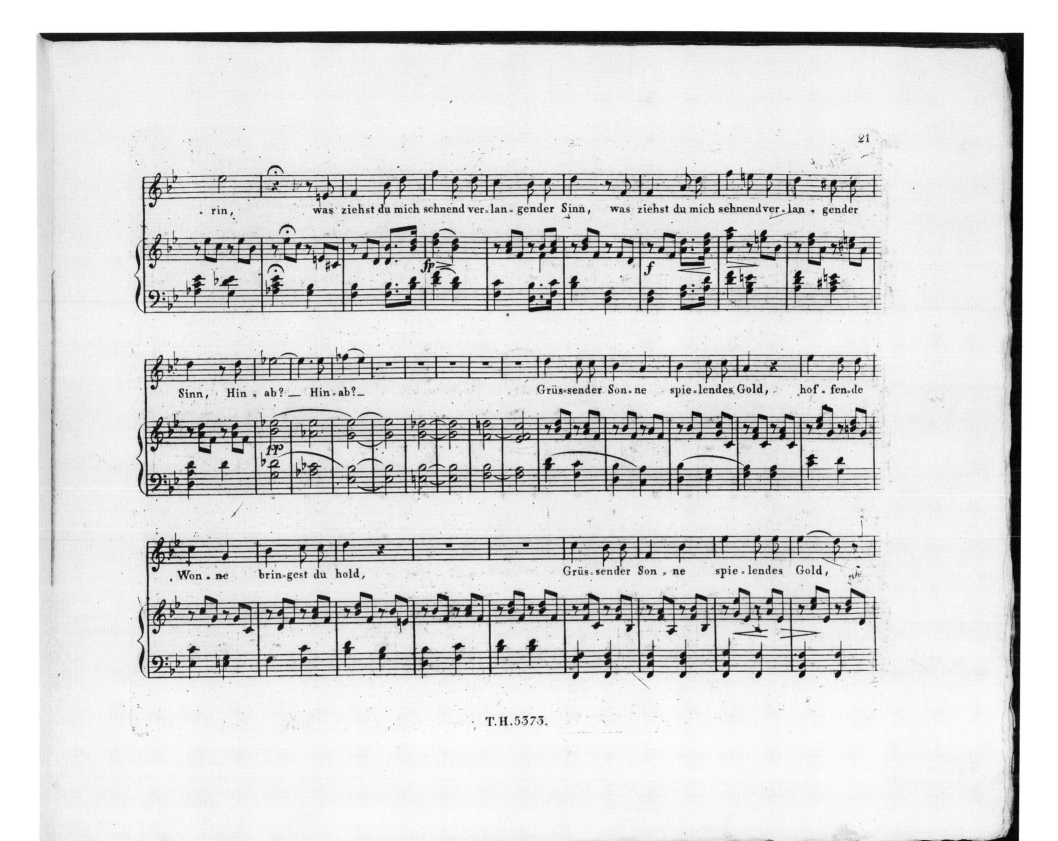

T.H.5373.

im=mer nur Thrä=nen, Kla=ge und Schmerz?   Auch ich bin mir schwellender Trie=be bewusst, wer

stil=let mir end=lich die drängende Lust?   Nur   du   be=freyst den Lenz in der Brust, nur du   be=

freyst den   Lenz in der Brust,   nur du __ __ nur du __ __ __!

T. H. 5373.

IV.

Ständchen,

von

FRANZ SCHUBERT.

———— ✳ ————

(5374.)

Eigenthum u. Verlag von Tob. Haslinger in Wien.

in des Mon=des Licht, des Verrä = thers feindlich Lau=schen fürchte, Hol = de, nicht, fürchte Hol = de

nicht.

Hörst die Nach = ti = gal=len schlagen? ach sie flehen dich,

T. H. 5374.

30

mit der Tö = ne süssen Kla = gen fle = hen sie für mich.

Sie verstehn des Busens Seh = nen, ken = nen Lie = bes schmerz, kennen Lie = bes schmerz, rühren mit den

Silber = tö = nen je = des wei = che Herz, je = des wei = che Herz. Lass auch dir die Brust be =

T.H.5374.

V.

Aufenthalt,

von

FRANZ SCHUBERT.

———————✱———————

(3375.)

Eigenthum u. Verlag von Tob. Haslinger in Wien.

"Aufenthalt," braces 1–3: mm. 1–7, 8–17, 18–26

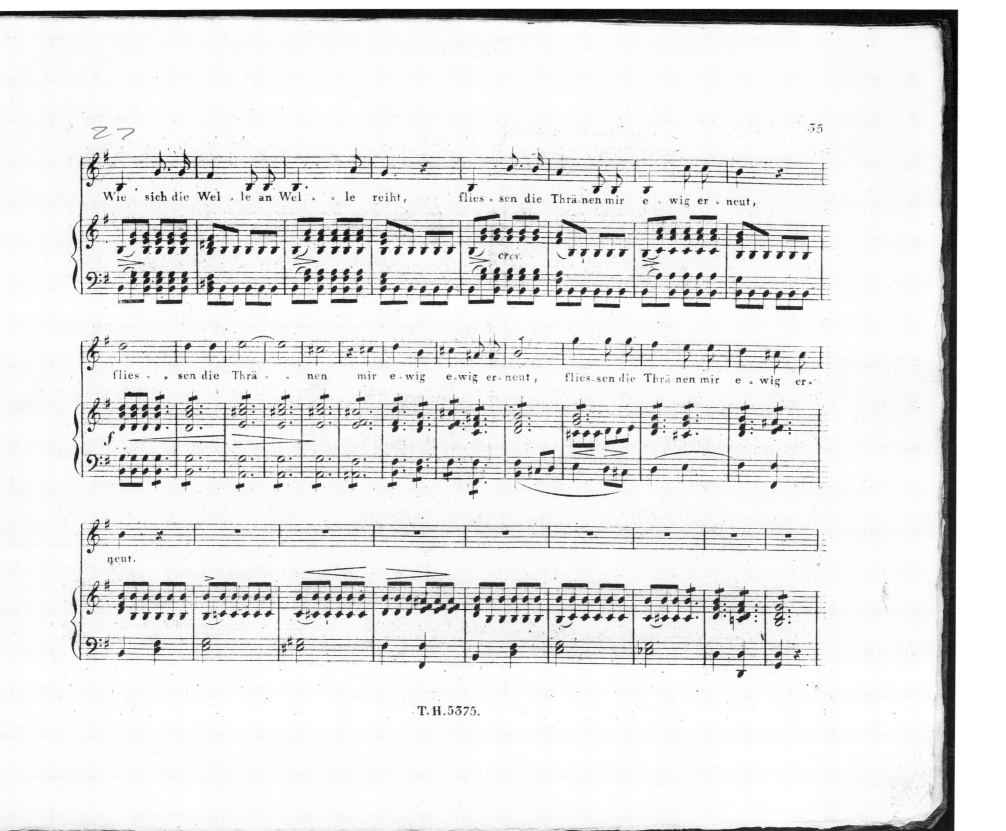

T. H. 5375.

"Aufenthalt," braces 1–3: mm. 56–66, 67–77, 78–85

T.H.5375.

VI.

In der Ferne,

von

FRANZ SCHUBERT.

———— ✳ ————

(5376.)
Eigenthum u. Verlag von Tob. Haslinger in Wien.

"In der Ferne," braces 1–3: mm. 1–8, 9–17, 18–27

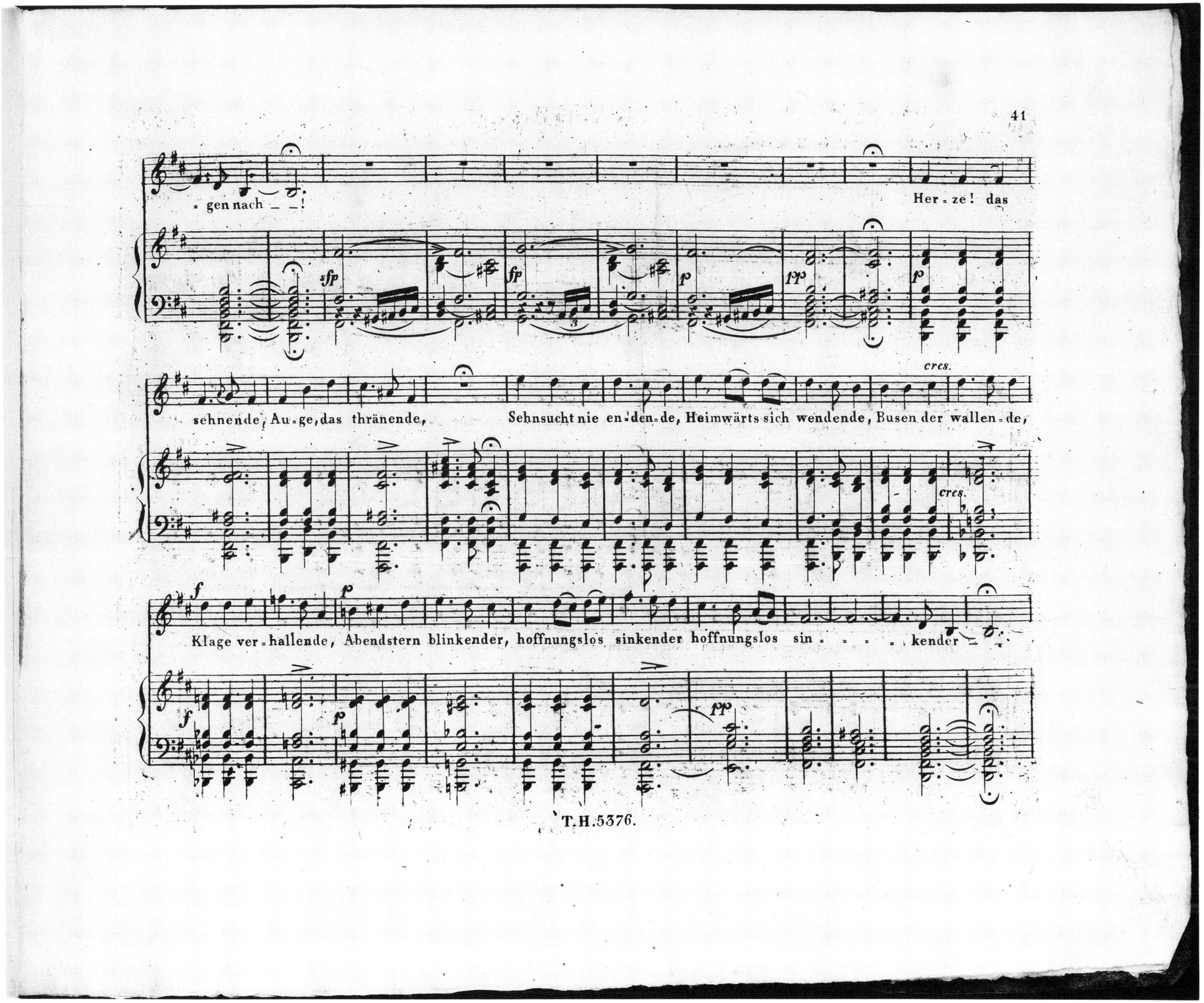

"In der Ferne," braces 1–3: mm. 28–37, 38–47, 48–58

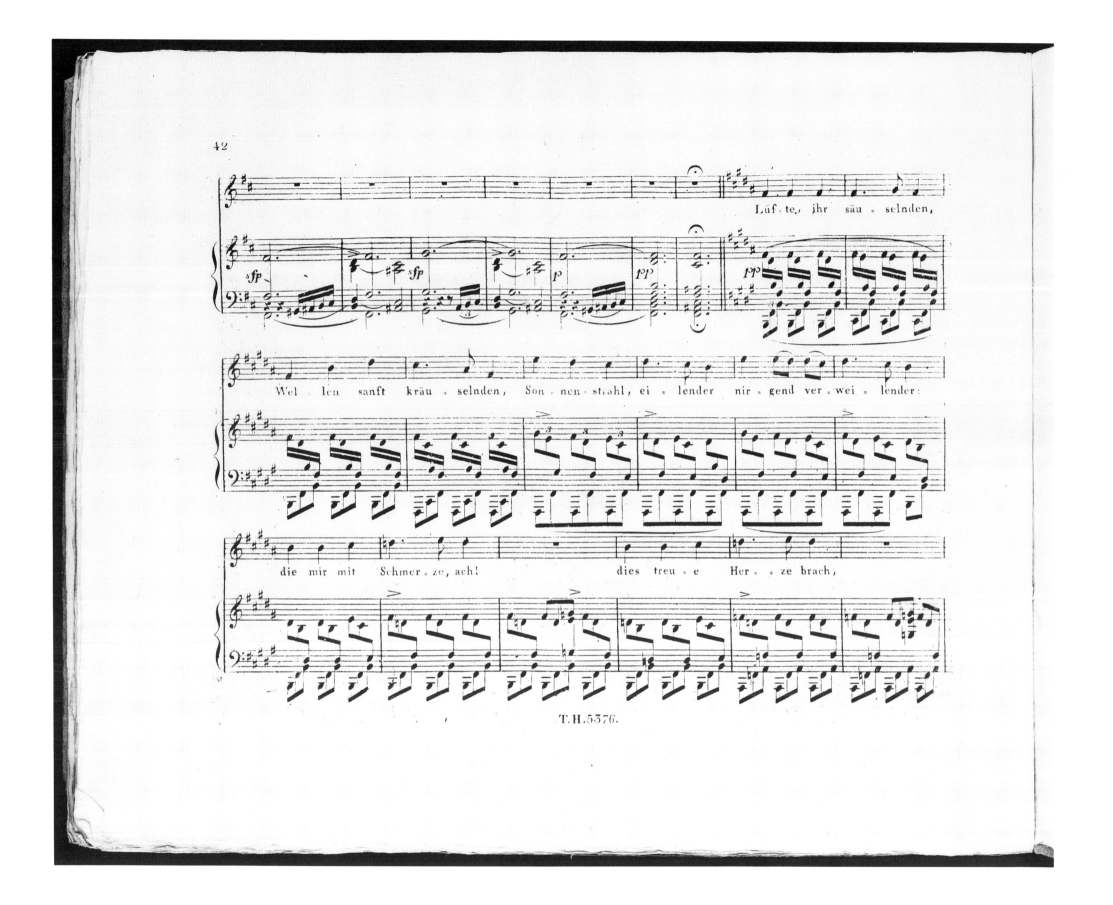

"In der Ferne," braces 1–3: mm. 59–67, 68–73, 74–79

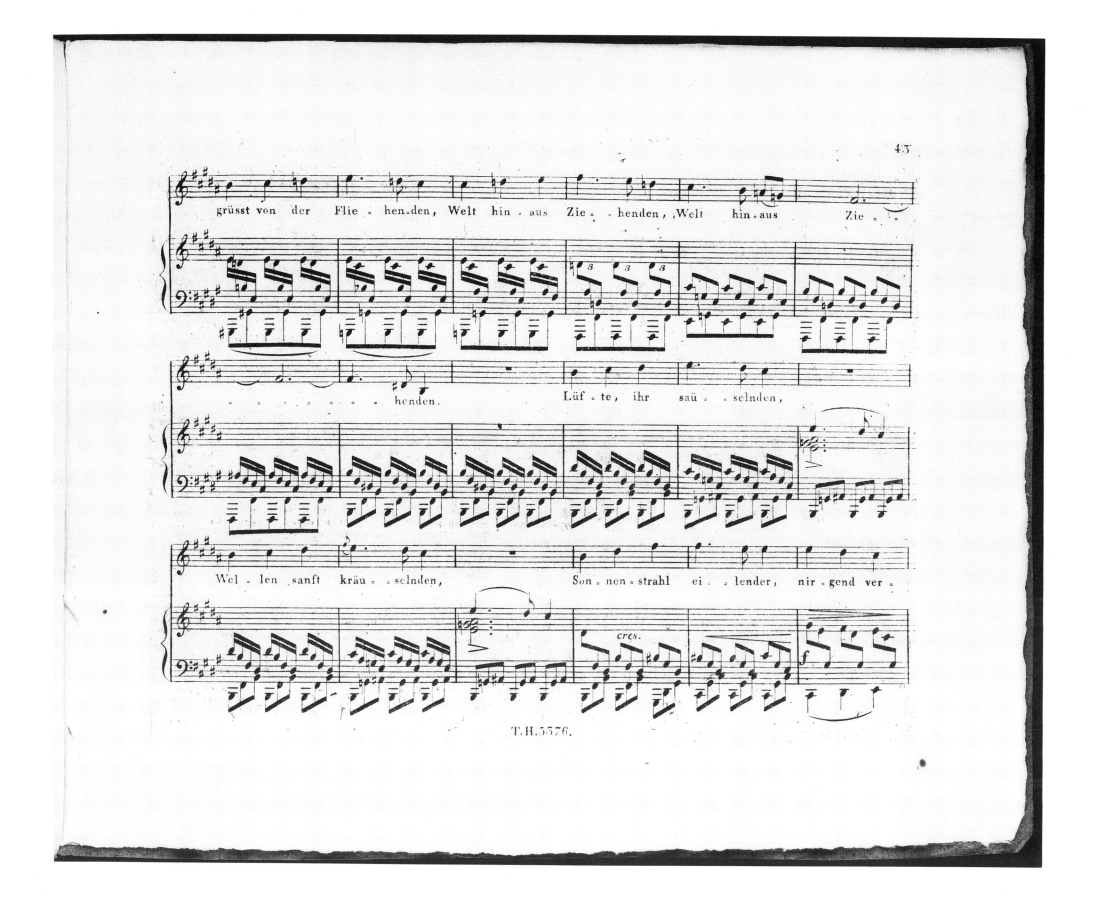

T. H. 5576.

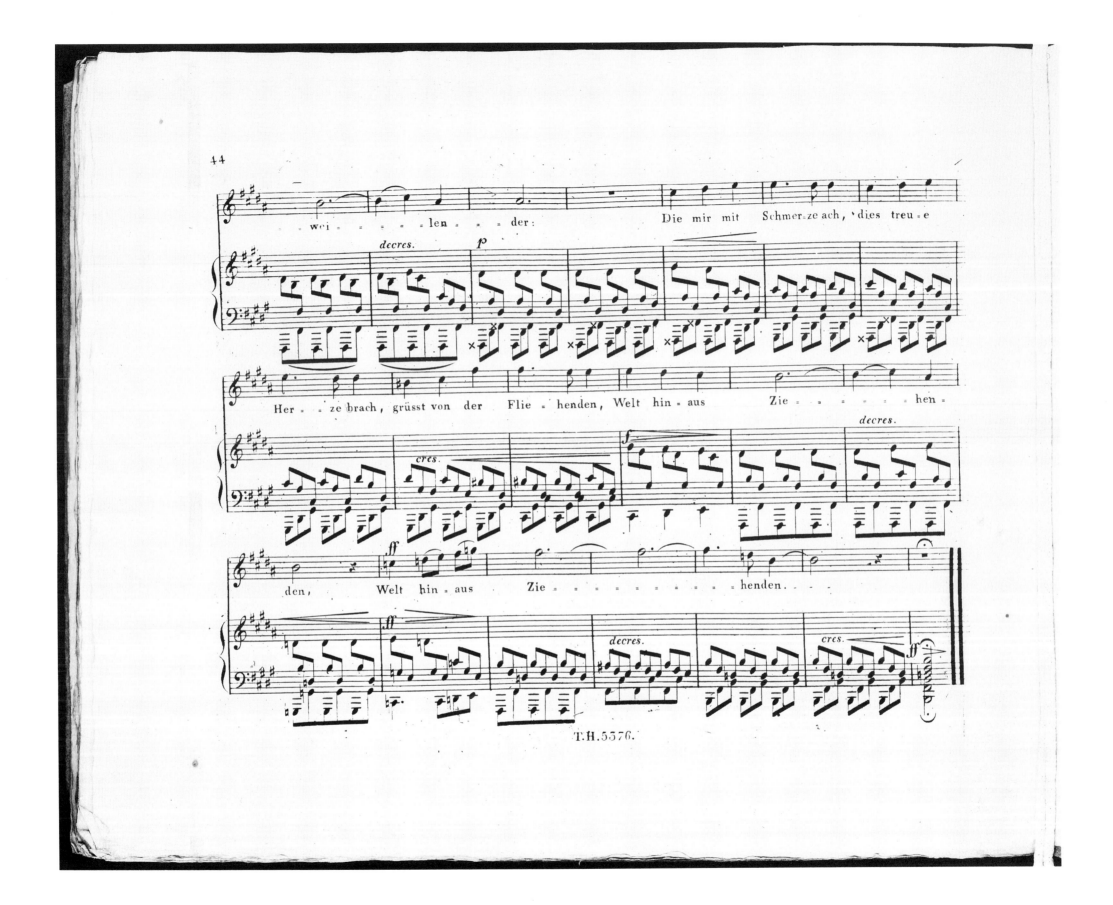

SCHWANEN-GESANG.

VON

Franz Schubert.

2te Abtheilung.

WIEN, BEI TOBIAS HASLINGER.

SCHWANENGESANG.

In Musik gesetzt

für eine Singstimme mit Begleitung des Pianoforte

von

Franz Schubert.

LETZTES WERK.

IIte Abtheilung.

N° 5570. Eigenthum des Verlegers. Preis f 3 C.M.

Wien, bey Tobias Haslinger,
Musikverleger,
im Hause der ersten österr: Sparkasse
am Graben N° 572.

INHALT.

————————— * —————————

T H 5371.

VII.

Abschied,

von

FRANZ SCHUBERT.

———— ✳ ————

(5377.)

Eigenthum u. Verlag von Tob. Haslinger in Wien.

"Abschied," braces 1–3: mm. 1–5, 6–11, 12–16

T.H.5377.

"Abschied," braces 1–3: mm. 33–38, 39–43, 44–48

"Abschied," braces 1–3: mm. 49–53, 54–59, 60–65   107

"Abschied," braces 1–3: mm. 66–70, 71–75, 76–81

T.H.5377.

"Abschied," braces 1–3: mm. 99–104, 105–110, 111–116

T.H.5377.

112   *"Abschied," braces 1–3: mm. 134–139, 140–144, 145–149*

T.H.5577.

VIII.

Der Atlas,

von

FRANZ SCHUBERT.

———— * ————

(5378.)

Eigenthum u. Verlag von Tob. Haslinger in Wien.

"Der Atlas," braces 1–3: mm. 1–5, 6–11, 12–17

60

stolzes Herz, und je = tzo bist du e = lend, Ich un = glücksel' = ger

cres.

Atlas, ich unglücksel'ger Atlas, die gan=zeWelt der Schmerzen muss ich tragen, die ganze Welt muss ich tra-gen, die

ganze Welt der Schmerzen muss ich tra = gen.

T.H.5378.

118   *"Der Atlas," braces 1–3: mm. 35–40, 41–48, 49–56*

IX.

Ihr Bild,

von

FRANZ SCHUBERT.

———— ✳ ————

(5379.)

Eigenthum u. Verlag von Tob. Haslinger in Wien.

"Ihr Bild," braces 1–3: mm. 1–6, 7–12, 13–18

X.

Das Fischermädchen,

von

FRANZ SCHUBERT.

———— * ————

(5380.)

Eigenthum u. Verlag von Tob. Haslinger in Wien.

"Das Fischermädchen," braces 1–3: mm. 1–6, 7–12, 13–18

T.H.5380.

täg-lich dem wil-den Meer, ver-traust du dich doch sorg = = los täglich dem wilden Meer.

täglich dem wilden Meer.

dim:

Mein Herz gleicht ganz dem Mee = re, hat Sturm und Ebb' und Fluth,

T. H. 5380.

"Das Fischermädchen," braces 1–3: mm. 37–42, 43–48, 49–54

T.H.5380.

XI.

Die Stadt,

von

FRANZ SCHUBERT.

———— ✳ ————

(5381.)

Eigenthum u. Verlag von Tob. Haslinger in Wien.

"Die Stadt," braces 1–3: mm. 1–3, 4–8, 9–14

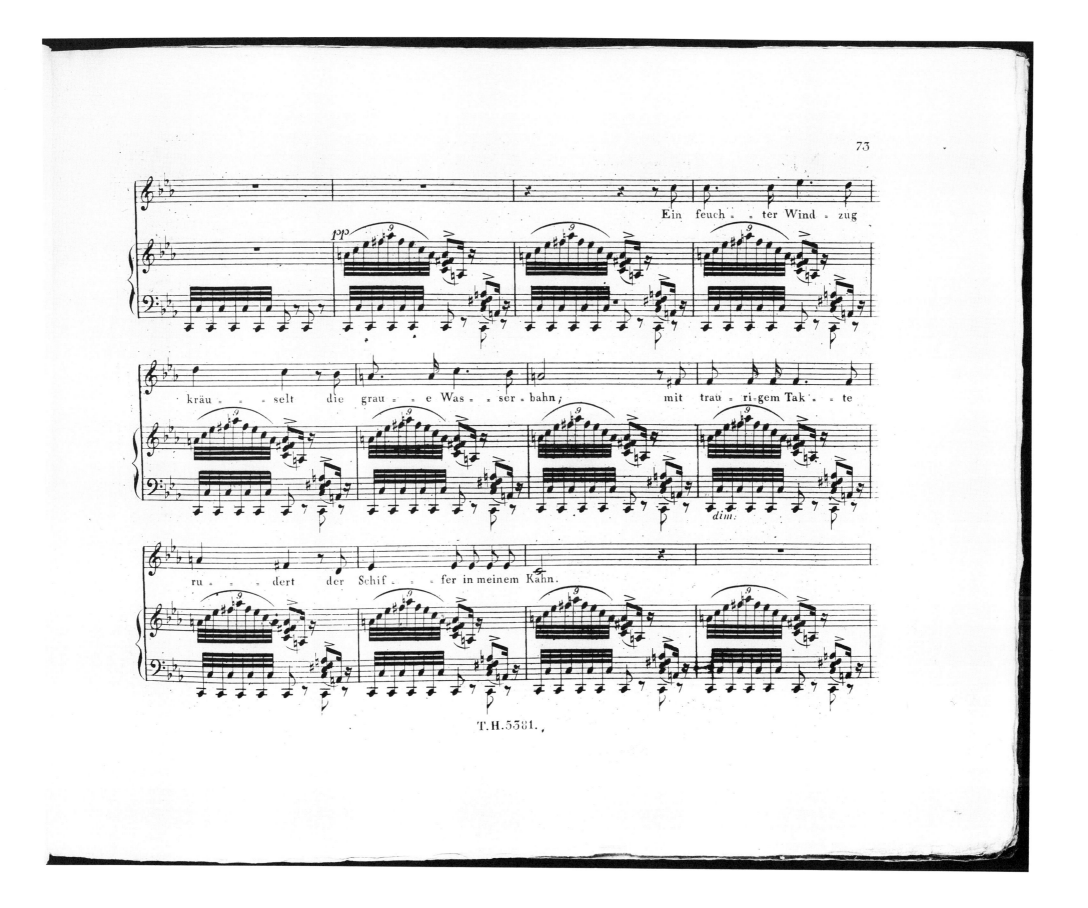

T.H.5381.

"Die Stadt," braces 1–3: mm. 27–31, 32–36, 37–40

XII.

Am Meer,

von

FRANZ SCHUBERT.

———— ✳ ————

(5582.)

Eigenthum u. Verlag von Tob. Haslinger in Wien.

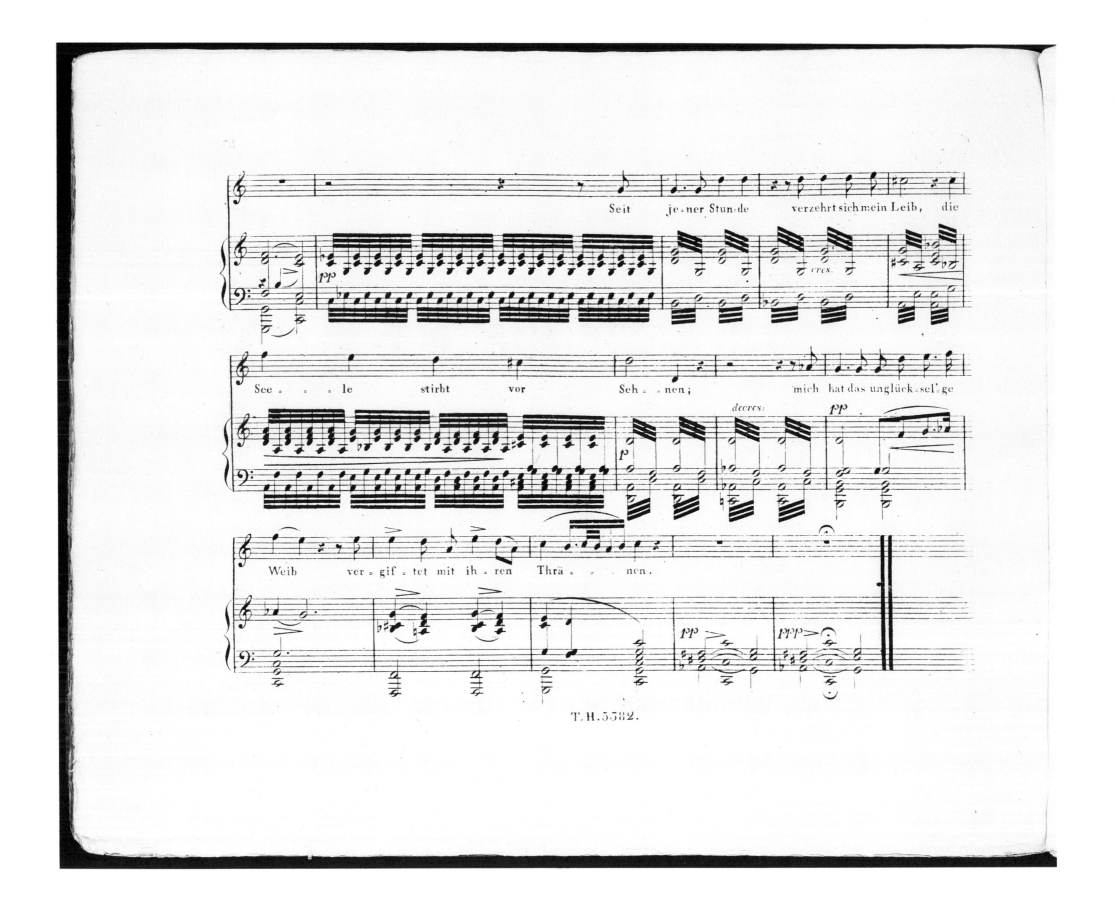

136   *"Am Meer," braces 1–3: mm. 32–36, 37–40, 41–45*

XIII.

Der Doppelgänger,

von

FRANZ SCHUBERT.

———————✳———————

(5383.)

Eigenthum u. Verlag von Tob. Haslinger in Wien.

"Der Doppelgänger," braces 1–3: mm. 1–7, 8–15, 16–22

T.H.5383.

140   *"Der Doppelgänger," braces 1–3: mm. 45–49, 50–56, 57–63*

XIV.

Die Taubenpost,

von

FRANZ SCHUBERT.

———— ✳ ————

(5384.)

Eigenthum u. Verlag von Tob. Haslinger in Wien.

"Die Taubenpost," braces 1–3: mm. 1–5, 6–11, 12–17

"Die Taubenpost," braces 1–3: mm. 36–41, 42–47, 48–53

T.H.5384.

"Die Taubenpost," braces 1–3: mm. 54–59, 60–65, 66–71   145

146   *"Die Taubenpost," braces 1–3: mm. 72–76, 77–82, 83–87*

Editorial Notes

THREE SKETCHES FOR *Schwanengesang*

"Liebesbotschaft": Measure numbers in parentheses are equivalent to those of the final version of the song.

"Liebesbotschaft," brace 1: Schubert intended the prelude, not yet written, to occupy this blank brace.

"Frühlingssehnsucht": The title, "Erster Entwurf zu Rellstabs 'Frühlingssehnsucht,'" was written by Eusebius Mandyczewski, chief editor of the old complete Schubert edition. He prepared all the song volumes in that publication.

"Die Taubenpost": Measure numbers in parentheses are equivalent to those of the final version of the song. Schubert had not yet written the prelude, therefore there are no measures to match (1–5).

"Die Taubenpost," mm. 75–78: These measures make up a keyboard interlude that Schubert eliminated from the final version of the song.

Schwanengesang: THE FIRST EDITION

"Frühlingssehnsucht," mm. 58–102: These measures constitute strophe 2 (the second of the five stanzas of the poetry) and are musically equivalent to mm. 13–57 (strophe 1). Schubert provides a single setting for stanzas 1–4 of the poetry (see the autograph). See also mm. 103–147 and mm. 148–192.

"Frühlingssehnsucht," mm. 103–147: These measures constitute strophe 3. See mm. 58–102.

"Frühlingssehnsucht," mm. 148–192: These measures constitute strophe 4. See mm. 58–102.

"Ständchen," mm. 37–60: These measures 37–60 constitute strophe 2 (the second of three stanzas of the poetry) and are musically equivalent to mm. 5–28 (strophe 1). Schubert provides a single setting for the first two stanzas (see the autograph).